Dark
Circle

*Carmen - Happy
Reading!
JPChoquette*

J.P. Choquette

This book is a work of fiction. All persons, events and details are products of the author's imagination or highly embellished facts.

The geographical location in which this novel is set is real, however liberties have been taken by the author as to specific places within the setting.

Dark Circle. Copyright © 2014 by J.P. Choquette. All rights reserved. Printed in the United States of America.

Library of Congress Cataloging-in-Publication Data

Dark Circle / Choquette, J.P.--1st CreateSpace Paperback ed.

ISBN-13: 9781494220334
ISBN-10: 1494220334

DEDICATION

For Maman and Papa,

Merci de m'avoir accepté comme l'un des vôtres.

On'saime

ACKNOWLEDGMENTS

Grateful thanks to the following people:

Aimee Perrino, proofreader divine (any leftover typos are my own).

Pam Irish and Wanda Baillargeon, for once again acting as early readers. Thank you for the encouragement and suggestions.

Cori Lynn Arnold, my critique partner, for your excellent insight. And all the other members of my Sisters in Crime family who consistently provide me with information and inspiration.

All the lovely readers of my first novel, *Epidemic*, who have been so supportive and kind.

And finally, Serge, thank you for continuing to believe.

~Dios Amore~

{Prologue}

Philadelphia, Pennsylvania

I tip the champagne glass up, light forming a prism as the last of the warm sourness slides into my mouth. My head is warm and thick, like a woolly blanket. The anger and tightness in my chest are gone. Disappeared two glasses before, to be honest.

The key scrapes in the lock, the heavy door swinging open and then the normal sounds in succession that Cole makes every time he arrives home. First, the clink of the keys hitting the silver dish by the door. Four steps and then the soft swoosh of the coat closet as he hangs his jacket and puts down his leather driving gloves. Fourteen steps across the great room where he flicks on the television, then a pause while he watches the stocks roll across the screen.

I set my glass in the marble sink of the cavernous kitchen and go back to arranging a bouquet of wildflowers for a still life. Commissioned six months ago to paint the piece, I've been struggling to find time between my studio and shop. I study the arrangement, remove an aster stalk and cut it shorter then wedge it between a lily and cornflower.

I'm about to replace the lily with a fiery orange Gerber daisy when my husband of five years slides his arms around my waist. I'd lost track of his progression into the kitchen. He nuzzles his cheek

3

into my neck. I stand as cold and rigid as a knife blade.

"What's the matter, darling?" He sighs, shoving away from the counter and moving to look into my face.

"Nothing," I mutter knowing fully how stupid that sounds. I might as well answer his question with "peanut butter," or "sky."

"I'm sorry . . . I'm late?" The statement that was a question. Typical Cole. "Is that it?"

"Bloody hell, Cole, what time is it?" My hands jerk away from the flowers and toward the huge face on the silver antique clock. "Eight o'clock. You were supposed to be here at six. Did you forget what day it is? You couldn't get in touch with me on one of your fifty-five electronic devices? How about a payphone? A gas station somewhere in Philadelphia must still have a payphone."

Cole steps back, raising his hands. "Woah. I get that you're irritated, but there's no need. I've got dinner covered. I didn't forget it's our anniversary, and I'm taking you out on the town." He smiles his winning client grin.

"I don't want to go out on the town," I reply, surprised the words are able to slither out through my clenched teeth. "I made Beef Wellington. And peas and new potatoes. And lemon torte. But that was at six o'clock when I thought you'd be home, and now everything is cold, and I have a painting to finish."

I sweep up the vase of flowers, clearing stems and flower bits into the trash on my way out of the room.

"Happy Anniversary," I say and let the kitchen door swing silently closed behind me.

I sit in my art studio for more than an hour but inspiration has run away with its tail between its legs. The tight ball in my chest has morphed, frustration making my legs jittery and my hands clench. Finally I sigh, put down the brush and dab at it with water, cleaning chartreuse paint from the bristles. The sink in the corner of my studio is splattered with the remains of previous projects. I turn, leaving the brush drying on the sideboard and look at the space.

My home studio has high ceilings, tall windows, pale yellow walls and bright pops of turquoise and orange which have become my signature. Geometric patterns on the curtains, black accents, and along nearly every wall, floor to ceiling shelving. Boxes are neatly labeled, but they don't need to be. I could find everything I need in this room with my eyes closed. When I opened my first brick and mortar store last year, I intended to work in a back room. But I spend so much time there already that this room has become my sacred space.

Guilt nibbles at my chest as I think about all the work Cole put into my store, into making it a success. My childhood dream became his in the years since we first met in England. He's not the first husband to have screwed up anniversary plans, I suppose. Some of the tenseness leaves my body, slinking off like a shadow. I smile, shut off the lights in the studio and close the door.

My hand trails along the chair rail down the hallway and into our bedroom. Cole is lying still in his work clothes, on top of the coverlet. His hair is mussed, chin dropped forward onto his chest. For a minute I imagine him as a little boy, exhausted after a long afternoon playing in the sandbox and chasing frogs.

The television anchorman is blathering on about the recent dip in the financial market. I click it off but Cole doesn't move. The tight ache in my chest loosens even more and I smooth back a piece of hair, kiss his forehead.

Following the wide staircase down to the first floor I find shoes, then keys. A quick drive will refresh me. I picture the rest of my frustration blowing out the open windows, cool air replacing what's left of the heat inside.

Windows down, I turn the volume up, and Ella Fitzgerald's voice works her magic, draining away the remaining tension. I drive aimlessly. Away from the lights of the city toward the flat roads that lead out of Philadelphia. Our little cul-de-sac becomes a distant point of light as I meander from one road to another. The air smells clean and warm, still tinged with the dampness of the rain from earlier today. I swerve to miss a leaping frog caught in the light beams of my Audi.

The blue lights catch me by surprise, so much that I nearly stop dead in the road.

Shit.

Gathering my wits, I steer off to the side, slowing and then letting the car purr to a full stop.

I reach into my handbag on the seat beside me, pull out a piece of peppermint gum and pop it into my mouth. Seconds pass, then I extract the registration and insurance paperwork from the glove box. The cop is sure to ask for it.

He emerges a moment later from the squad car. He's short, muscular, broad shouldered and walks with a swagger. I roll my eyes before he gets to my window. Typical power-hungry rookie, I think.

But his face is older than I imagined as he leans down close to me.

"Evening, ma'am."

"Good evening, officer," I reply. My voice sounds steady despite the fast thumping under my ribs.

He looks me over and I shiver. I recognize that look. Not one of keen observation but something dark. I glance behind us. The road stretches, black and empty behind. My heart beats faster.

"Is there a problem?" I ask. This time my voice sounds a bit breathless.

"Depends," the officer says. Correction: sergeant. *Sergeant Melvin Brooks* it says on a gold bar over his breast pocket. "You been drinking?"

"Drinking?" My voice has raised an octave. I take a deep breath then another. *Steady, Sarah. Slow down.*

"Just a bit," I say. "A glass of champagne. For my anniversary."

"Really? Just one glass." Sergeant Brooks sounds like I've just told him the world is flat or that the road we're on is actually constructed from cheese. He chuckles. The sound is rusty.

"Get out of the car, please, ma'am."

Is this standard procedure? Doesn't he just need to run my information? Questions form, but my brain refuses to process them. Instead I'm faced with little empty holes where answers should be.

He opens the door without waiting for my reply. I fumble with my seatbelt, and he chuckles again. Then I scoot out, pulling my skirt down and smoothing it as I do. The road behind us remains dark, deserted. I look at the cop again, and panic fills my throat.

"Beautiful night, isn't it?" He says unexpectedly, glancing above us at the trees that frame this stretch of road.

For an instant I think I'm wrong. That my instincts are off, dulled by the champagne and my imagination, which has been playing tricks on me again. I glance up, too and see that he's right. The trees are backlit by a sliver of moon. Frogs peep in a swampy area nearby, and I hear a shrill call of an insect that I can't remember the name of.

But then his hands are iron tight around my arms, and I'm pinned against the car. His breath is hot on my neck and face and smells of onions and stale cigarettes. And I think I'm going to be sick, but his mouth is so close to mine that I feel dizzy. Ella's finished her song and Billie Holliday is crooning a tune I can't quite remember the name of.

{Chapter One}

St. Albans, Vermont

Her name is Charlotte and she speaks quickly, hands moving like thin birds in front of her. She pauses only for a moment to take a miniscule sip of her coffee and then starts right back in, barely pausing for breath.

Charlotte is the first neighbor in the community to introduce herself. In fact, in the three months that Cole and I have lived at Hawthorne Estates, she's one of the only people I've seen. Her property sits kitty corner to ours, separated by the tall, voluptuous hedges common in gated communities. When I'd mentioned to Cole how odd it was we hadn't seen anyone out in their yards, he'd shrugged it off.

"It's winter, Sarah. In Vermont, mid-March is the time to huddle up and wait out the rest of the cold weather. What did you expect, cross country skiers on the main drive?" He'd smiled when he'd said it, teasing me.

". . . and that's when we moved here," Charlotte says, pausing again for a doll-sized sip of coffee. I wonder if I put in too much cream and sugar. She looks as though she hasn't had either in years.

I smile, take a sip from my own cup, and lean forward in my chair.

"I'm so glad you took the initiative, Charlotte, to come for a visit," I say. "I've been thinking of baking bread for all the neighbors just as an excuse to introduce myself."

"Oh." She looks alarmed. I wonder if it's the thought of eating bread or my showing up on the doorstep unannounced that's cause for concern.

"I hope you won't let our unfriendliness bother you. We're not really so bad, just busy with work and social engagements. You know how that goes." Charlotte smiles brightly.

I nod and smile, but I can't actually remember how it felt. My days now are long and slow. And tedious. For an instant I remember the long, black days that spooled out like ribbon—the ones after the hospital—but I block the memory out and take another sip of coffee.

"Can I get you something else? A slice of blueberry bread? Lemon cake?"

Charlotte waves off both, another worried look marring her unlined face. *It was the bread, then.*

"Thanks, but no. I'm on a strict no-carb diet. Marc has his business bash in the Caribbean in a few weeks, and I need to be able to fit into my bikini and impress the partners' wives." She laughs, joking. I smile back but think that if she loses any more weight she might not find a swimsuit tiny enough to fit. At least not in the adult section of the store.

"Forgive me, Sarah. I've been completely monopolizing the conversation. Tell me more about you and your husband. Is it Cole?"

"It is, yes." I freeze for a moment, unable to think of how to work around the hospitalization, unable to remember momentarily what it was that I used to do in my other life the one where I was competent and confident. The life where I was actually me.

"I'm an artist," I blurt out. This at least is true, though I haven't taken up a brush in months. "Originally from London. I met Cole seven years ago while he was working there; two years later we married. We just moved here from Philadelphia, where we lived for a while."

"Oh, London," Charlotte says, her eyes looking dreamily out the window. "I loved it there. I had such a lovely time exploring Europe when Marc was opening some large accounts in Paris."

Marc, I'd learned, was in financial securities, though what he actually did with money I wasn't exactly sure.

"London is lovely," I agree. "Of course, I'm biased."

"Do you miss it?"

I pause but just for a moment.

"Yes."

"What do you miss the most?" Charlotte sets her coffee cup down carefully and rests her tiny hands on the top knee of her long slender legs that are crossed in front of her.

I close my eyes, just for a moment, then look past her out the massive wall of windows that makes up one-half of our kitchen.

"I miss my kitchen. It was small and outdated and butter yellow, and I completely loved it. It was horrible, really. A mess of dangerous wiring and shorts that would make an electrician roll in his grave."

Charlotte laughs.

"I miss afternoon tea. Not the tea itself. You can get that anywhere. But the ritual of it. It was so comforting. And silly things you take for granted like the mechanical voice on the tube saying, "Mind the gap," a thousand times a day. I miss chocolate shops: real chocolate shops where they hand dip their sweets, and the smell slips out the shop windows and doors and into the street. And I miss Christmas when carolers dress up like characters in a Charles Dickens story and wander around the streets singing. It was so magical."

I stop and force a chuckle.

"I'm sorry. I'm going on and on like some smarmy advertisement. Vermont is beautiful. Lovely. It really is. I'm sure that in time I'm going to love it here. It's so . . ." I search for the right word. "Tranquil. And natural."

"And tediously boring," Charlotte says and laughs.

"No, really, it's breathtaking and lovely in its own way."

Charlotte rolls her eyes.

"I've lived here for many years, and I still can't get used to the weather. I suppose as a flatlander—that's the term the natives use for any of us who haven't tilled the soil for the past two hundred years—I will someday come to appreciate it. At least that's what Marc tells me. I'm not so sure."

Charlotte stands, her chair gliding soundlessly away from the table. We're seated in the dining room, the least-used room in the house. When Charlotte stands a shadow passes the sun and the room is momentarily dimmed, gray walls turning dark and dingy, white porcelain dishes in the high china cabinet looking brittle. I shiver, rubbing my hands over my arms.

"That's another reason to take a mid-winter break," Charlotte says, pointing at my arms. "It's a chance to remember that there is indeed a sun still up there in the sky somewhere."

I walk her through the long hall toward the front door. Her heels click on the tile, making tapping sounds. I pad behind her, stocking feet soundless. The sun peers out again as I open the thick glass-paned door. The handle is iron and twisted, it feels heavy and awkward in my hand. Cumbersome, smothering. Like this house and neighborhood. I push the thought away, clear my throat.

"Thanks again for stopping," I tell Charlotte. *Should I give her a hug? An air kiss? A handshake, maybe?* She resolves the dilemma for me by tapping quickly down the stairs, donning her jacket as she moves, pushing arms into a fluff of baby blue fur.

"Seal," she says, smoothing it over her and zipping the coat to her chin. "Baby seal," she whispers with her finger pressed coquettishly to her lips. "But don't tell. You never know when there might be an animal rights activist in our midst." She laughs, and the sound is as tight and tinkling as she is, sharp and pointed in the cold air.

I force a polite smile, pushing the thought of sweet, fuzzy, white seals out of my mind and close the door halfway behind me. Charlotte waves thin fingers in my direction.

"Great to meet you, Sarah," she says and then slips behind the wheel of the extra-large SUV ("Seating for seven!" she'd remarked earlier) and backs quickly from the curved driveway. With another wave, she passes onto the main drive, leading to the town highway beyond.

Charlotte is desperately in need of more warm weather clothes, she said, and it is miles and miles to the nearest women's specialty shop. The marble steps are icy beneath my feet, but I stand for another few minutes, sucking in the fresh, cold air and dull sunshine like a drowning woman. Then I turn and walk back into the house, heavy door closing behind me like a coffin.

{Chapter Two}

Leaves encrusted under a thin layer of ice crackle beneath my boots as I walk. The forest behind our home is magnificent, dense and wild. Animal sightings are frequent: deer, rabbits, foxes, and the ever tweeting songbirds. This morning it's louder than ever, nearly deafening as though I am walking in a rain forest instead of through New England hardwood and pines.

I make a mental note to look for a birding book next time I'm at the library. I've been spending hours in the woods and it would be nice to learn at least some of the calls from my feathered friends. Thinking of the birds makes me think of Charlotte. I picture her at this moment, wandering through a ritzy women's store, waving her hands at the sales women to bring alligator sandals and calf-hair bags, and while they are at it, baby kitten-fur lined coats into the dressing room.

To each her own, though the thought of baby animals being killed to make a fashion statement turns my stomach. A particularly loud bird caws overhead. A crow. That one I recognize. The air is fresh, and the cold aches my lungs. It's a welcome discomfort, and I expand my chest, drawing the scent of pine needles, loamy soil and sweet, decayed leaves deeper inside.

When I come to the woods, I make a pledge with myself not to dwell on negative things. I think instead about color and patterns, shape and contrast. Mother Nature is the ultimate creative.

The gravel path is hard. The bits that must be loose in summer are stuck firmly together with frost and ice, packed into a cement-like material. I adjust my hat, pulling it slightly off my ears to feel the sun. There's a quarrel going on in the treetops above me. Seconds later an agitated squirrel skitters down the trunk of a huge pine tree and leaps across the path, then into the forest on the other side. The party left behind makes another screeching sound but stays hidden in the tree. Apparently even animals aren't immune to daily drama and office politics.

The path ahead curves, following a brook to my right. Snow covers most of the area, which is indented. I continue left, realizing after a few moments that I've never been this deep into the woods. The path comes to a "V." The right side is covered in gravel, but the left, I realize, is more of a dirt path. A niggling voice tells me that it would be safer to stay on the main walking path. Ignoring it, I give in to my curiosity and go left.

The woods become thicker, the animal sounds, quieter. Everything here is quieter, hushed and muffled by ancient pine boughs and layer upon layer of dead leaves that have composted into thick, soft down lining the forest floor.

I'm lost in thought when I see something that stops my boots mid-stride. Sunlight, tarnished yellow, trickles through the thick branches overhead illuminating a figure in the woods. Or is it a tree? I squint, too far away to see clearly. I walk more slowly, trying to quiet my feet and the breath in my lungs which suddenly sounds deafening.

More steps, quiet, slow. The path before me twists, and I'm left, abruptly in a large, open clearing. I look again to the spot where I think I saw the figure. The hair along my neck rises, and my breath stops in my throat. The loud song of the birds is drowned out by the louder throb of my heartbeat. I blink my eyes once, twice. An illusion, maybe?

But it's not.

Silhouetted against a backdrop of thick, rough trees is a woman.

A gray woman.

A ghost.

Immobile and standing arrow straight between two maple trees. One hand rests against a tree trunk, as gnarled and rough looking as the bark. Gray hair, pulled back. A few pieces across her cheeks. Hard looking face. She wears a pale dress which reminds me of the buttery leather saddle bags I had when I took horseback riding lessons as a kid. She is slight but not skinny. Her face is turned, looking out across the clearing, her gaze intense. Then suddenly her head turns and she's staring at me. Face angry, eyes, narrowing. Without thinking I suck in my breath. A tree branch groans nearby, and I glance away, then back.

She's gone.

Goose bumps skitter up and down my arms and back then down my legs to my feet. I look again, checking the spot, then tracing my eyes left and right, but she's vanished.

A breath trapped and forgotten in my chest falls out, and I draw in another, then another, fast, quick. I stand for several more minutes, watching, but see nothing other than the trees, hear nothing but the incessant call of birds.

I don't remember retracing my steps through the woods or crossing from the forest to the maintained web of trails in the community, following one back to the house. I don't remember taking off my boots or putting on the tea kettle, but I hear it scream now and jump, hip bumping hard into the granite counter. I pour a steaming stream into a mug filled with a double shot of bourbon with shaking hands.

It isn't until I've drained the first cup of tea and am working on the second, that I come to my senses. I walk quickly into my studio, flipping the light switch and flooding the area with bright, natural light. I've lost my tea somewhere, but it doesn't matter. I can't do what I need to now without free hands.

Moving fast, I find a large sketch pad and a packet of charcoal pencils. With quick, uneven strokes I fill the page with images of the woman. My hands are still trembling slightly as I work, quickly finishing the first page and starting a second. My wrist and fingers begin to ache halfway through the third sketch. It's been months since I've used drawing implements, and my body is out of practice. Ignoring the discomfort, I hunch further forward and concentrate on the lines and details before I forget, capturing an image on paper that will come to matter more to me than I could ever imagine.

Three hours later I sip my first glass of wine, admiring the clarity of the pale yellow liquid in the glass backlit by a crackling fire. I sigh contentedly, moving closer to Cole on the wide couch.

"Good day?" he asks, muting the TV and looking at me. He's so handsome. The sharp planes of his face are made smoother by the shadows and firelight dancing off of them.

"Sure," I say, burrowing my head into the crook of his neck. He smells of cedar and aftershave, a sharp but pleasant smell. I nuzzle his neck, and he lifts a hand and smooths back my dark curls.

We sit quietly for a few moments before I sigh again.

"You sure it was a good day?" He tips my face toward him. I hesitate, and he notices.

"What is it?" he asks.

I draw back for a moment, drain the rest of my glass and balance the leggy stem on the coffee table.

"I saw something, or someone I should say, in the woods."

Silence.

Then, "Like a vagrant?"

"No." I pause, look out the wide bay of windows across the great room. The dark presses in so hard I can't see a speck of light outside.

"A woman. A…," I'm about to say "ghost" but then think better of it. "An elderly woman."

"In the woods. Alone?" Cole asks.

I nod.

"Did she look, you know, stable? Do you think she'd wandered away from home?"

I see her clearly in my mind: straight, gray, angry.

"No, I don't think so. She was old, but her eyes…" I shiver, look away from the window and back toward the fire. "Her eyes were sharp, clear. I don't think she was misplaced."

"Hmmm," Cole said, un-muting the television set. "You didn't recognize her though?"

"I didn't. Not that I know anyone around here yet. I mean, out in the greater community," I hurriedly add that last part, knowing that Cole is sensitive to our new neighborhood and more sensitive to the slights I've made regarding its unfriendly occupants.

We watch the screen in silence for another half hour before I give Cole a kiss and turn in. I take one more look at the sketches in my studio before getting into bed. They were quickly done, but the detail is good.

I bring one of the sheets closer, the one in which I drew her clothing. It was an instant glance in the woods, but later, when I was drawing, I didn't have to stop and think back about it. I knew. My hand and brain were working together so quickly that my mind didn't have a chance to get in the way. That's when my art is best, when my mind is left completely out of it.

What I see now on the paper starts a slow tremble in my hands. Fear or excitement? I'm not sure. I look at the sheet, look away. I scan my art room, wondering if there was something in it that I saw seconds before drawing, if that thing could have influenced this work. I take in the same cream-colored walls, the dark walnut wood trim, the wall of open shelves, antique locker baskets holding supplies and the long, scarred and paint-covered work table. But there's nothing. I never display artwork in my studio: mine or anyone else's. Too easy for it to influence future pieces. I look at the sketches again, then the room around me, eyes searching for any type of fabric, beads or odds and ends that would have made it into this piece. But again, nothing.

Looking at the sketch again, I hardly believe what I see. The woman's clothing is simple, but old. Ancient, maybe. The dress, buttery soft, pale yellow, is made from a soft, flexible material, most likely leather. There are bands of beads around the hem and neck, fringe hangs from the body of the dress itself, and though no patterns in the beadwork show in my sketch, I know they're there. This ghost has an identity. She's Native American.

Hurriedly, I take out the first sketch again, the one in which I captured her face and stance. Sharp, clear eyes stare out from a lined face. What color were the eyes? From the distance I was standing it was impossible to tell. The face itself has the beautiful high cheekbones of a native. I can see it now, and it's so obvious that I feel stupid for having missed it earlier. Her hair, which I just remembered was long, was behind her, but a few gray wisps moved around her face. Could it have been braided? I look the drawing over again and again, but no other details stick out at me.

What is an old, Native American ghost doing in our woods? I look out the bank of windows in my studio but am met once again with complete blackness. I move toward the door of the studio, turn out the light, then press my face against the glass like I did as a little girl.

It takes several minutes for my eyes to adjust, and once they do I can still see little. Dark rims of the patio and outbuildings appear just slightly darker than the night, which is lit only by a thin rind of moon and a handful of dim stars. I look toward the forest and see movement. The trees sway slightly in a breeze I can neither feel nor hear. For a moment I feel trapped inside a box of stone and glass. As though instead of keeping the night and cold and unknown out, I'm the one being held away in this beautiful, icy chest. I shiver again and hurry to my bedroom, crawling quickly between the sheets and blankets. I try to blot out the image of the woman and the icy branches and the feeling that somehow, someway this house is trying to imprison me.

{Chapter Three}

I drop Cole off at the airport in Burlington at 11:00 the next morning. Coming from London and the maze that's Heathrow, the airport in Vermont's largest city is simple, small and easy to maneuver. Within the last decade, the airport has undergone considerable expansion and renovations leaving me to wonder about the prior size. I'm familiar now with the parking garage and layout of the terminal, so that leaving Cole isn't the worry it was the initial time we'd attempted it. That first experience left me in tears, partly because I was all alone in this strange, new place, and partly out of fear of maneuvering icy roads or even getting out of the parking garage in one piece. Contrary to popular belief, it does take a bit of time and effort to re-learn to drive on the opposite side of the road. Bully for me, I did it.

A right onto the main drag brings me onto Williston Road. I adjust the heat and turn the radio off. I need to think. A sip of locally roasted, organic mocha helps me relax further. The airport is filled with local products, one of the things that Vermont is passionate about. "Buy Vermont," and "Buy Local" bumper stickers plaster cars and trucks and SUVs on city and country roads both. I take another sip of the drink and glance in the rearview mirror. The sketches, tucked in my art bag in the backseat, are my mission today. Or rather, the woman in them.

Seeing the ghost or woman or whoever she is unnerved me, but I'm also strangely grateful. It's taken my mind off the strange coldness of the house, the oddity of our completely unfriendly-bordering-on-hostile neighbors and the discomforting sensation I have every time I pass through the gate of our gated community.

Artists, it's been said, are spiritual floaters. Part of us, our psyche maybe, remains on a plane somewhere between earth and heaven. We're highly attuned to sensations and feelings, almost able to see and touch the emotions in a room.

Even though I've been an artist as long as I can remember, I still make a constant effort to temper my feelings. Because along with the sensations and heightened emotions creative types have comes the imagination which can so often lead where you don't want to go. It causes boogey men in the closets to appear real, monsters in the dark an anticipated norm rather than fairy tale. Creativity is both blessing and curse.

I shiver as I look out at the gray March morning, and move the heat dial a little higher. Thinking of boogey men and monsters reminds me of the Dark Time. That's what Cole and I refer to it as, on those very infrequent occasions we speak of it. Memories from that period come to me in snatches of visceral sensations: my hands, ice cold, fingertips rough and raw from bitten down nails, muffled sounds and voices, as though the world outside me was covered in a thick, downy layer of snow. I remember the sleeplessness and then the doctor overcompensating and the hibernation period, when I would try to rouse myself but constantly be pulled back under. Someone praying by my bedside. A cross on the wall opposite the ugly green chair where I'd sit for hours. The awful smell of overcooked hospital food and always the underlying scent of disinfectant.

A horn blasts. I've drifted into the middle line on Interstate 89.

"Bugger." I correct the wheel and give a small wave to the SUV roaring past. The driver doesn't look my way. Turning on the local public radio station, I catch the end of the national news before restful strains of Beethoven begin. Another few sips of mocha grounds me in the present, and the rest of my return drive north is uneventful.

St. Albans, a former railway town, is still a stop, however small, on Amtrak lines. The railway also sees a large number of freight trains carrying wood chips back and forth from Canada to Burlington for use as fuel. The town and city, split into two separate towns in 1902, make up the largest population in Franklin County at just over 14,000 residents. St. Albans, purportedly named after a Roman soldier who was killed for sheltering a Christian priest, morphed over time from flourishing railway hub to manufacturing mecca. The largest employers in the area consist of a pharmaceutical company, a chocolate factory, a ceramic machine parts company and Ben & Jerry's ice cream.

Today I'm headed to the historical society, housed in the city's pretty downtown area. I nose the Lexus into a parking spot behind the building which is flanked by two churches. The one to my right is painted red brick, the one on my left is a stone structure with a high steeple. At just the moment I open the car door, bells ring out. I smile. The sound is clear, and when I close my eyes I imagine that it's the early 1800s and instead of a car, I stand near a horse and wagon. The vision is so real that I'm somewhat surprised when I open my eyes and look down to see my knee-length coat and black pants instead of petticoats and an ankle-length dress.

Stepping through the glass foyer of the historical society only reiterates the feeling. I'm met with a full display of clothing and military accoutrements from the 18th and 19th centuries. The building is made up of three floors, two of which house memorabilia from the past and the top one which a sign tells me is taken up entirely by Bliss Auditorium. A map in the foyer points me to the office of the building's director, and I follow a maze through glass cases to her office.

A small plastic clock on the closed door tells me Paulette Bougeois is expected in ten minutes. I wonder if I'm alone in the building but then see a maintenance worker pushing a mop bucket ahead of him down a hall to my right. I call out good morning, then see white wires running from his ears, his head moving to music I can't hear.

Walking through the aisles of display cases my nose twitches from dust motes. The shelves are dust-free behind the glass though, every item tidy and amazingly well-preserved. Neatly typed signs describe the contents of various items. I laugh when I read one that describes a bed pan as a "relief tray." A relief to whoever used it, that's for sure.

My watch tells me that Paulette should be in though I haven't heard any doors open. I walk back toward her office in a circular path, peering in cases along the way. I bend over, looking at an antique tie tack supposedly worn by President Chester A. Arthur, one of two Vermonters who served in the Oval Office. The tack is dull and unimpressive. As I start to straighten I feel a presence behind me. The janitor, maybe? The hair along my neck creeps upward, and I look to the right and then left.

There's no one.

I face the case again and see a woman looking back at me in the glass who is not me. I jump, then turn awkwardly to look behind me. The woman from the woods, the ghost stares back at me, not four feet from where I'm standing. She's years younger but I recognize her ultra-straight posture, the dark, wild eyes and beautiful cheek bones.

My mind is working quickly, trying to put disjointed pieces together to make sense of what I'm seeing. I feel the tree branches scratching at my skin, my right heel rubbing against the inside of my boot where my sock slipped down, the smell of sunshine and fresh pine.

And fear.

I remember now my retreat from the woods yesterday, and though I couldn't see her then, I could feel her eyes on my back, staring, watching.

Waiting.

{Chapter Four}

"Can I help you?"

I yelp.

"I'm sorry. I thought you'd heard me come in," a woman stands two feet away. "My name is Paulette Bougeois. I'm the director here at the Society." She is petite, dark-haired and approaches me with her hand outstretched.

"I . . ." my voice wavers. I glance behind me again and see the straight gray woman staring back, directly into the glass case.

"Ah, you've met Josie, I see."

"Josie?" I swallow, throat dry.

"Josie Little Fish. I'm sure that wasn't her birth name, but it's the name she likely died with."

I involuntarily take a step backward, elbows bumping the display case behind me.

Paulette laughs, a surprisingly hearty sound.

"Don't worry, that's not really her. Just a wax replica."

I exhale and move forward slightly, peering into the perfectly-formed face.

"Are you sure?"

"Very. Why don't you come take a seat in my office for a moment? You look a little pale."

I accept the offer gratefully and follow Paulette's straight back to her office.

"I'm still getting used to our new hours," she explains while plugging in a white electric tea kettle. "I must have left the back door unlocked accidently. It's fine though," she smiles, when I begin to apologize. "Hank is around here somewhere, and I just ran down to Main Street to drop something off at the Chamber office for an event we're having next week. Tea?"

Several minutes later, sipping the hot drink, I glance around the director's office as she excuses herself to unlock the front doors and display a flag to let visitors know the Historical Society is officially open. The office is neat and tidy, like the woman. There are small stacks of relics, but each is tagged, labeled carefully and tucked into neat piles with the largest items at the bottom. Her office has original wainscoting and the large windows common in old buildings. Her desk is not empty, but all the office supplies and books are arranged in a way that tells me Paulette knows where each and every item is. The wood floor is old and worn but polished to a shine.

She returns, rubbing her hands together.

"Are you feeling better, Ms. . . I'm sorry, I just realized I don't know your name."

"Much better. Thank you." I smile and in fact, I do feel better. Enough to even feel a bit silly for the way I nearly swooned in the other room.

"I'm Sarah. Sarah Solomon," I say. "Pleased to meet you."

"It's good to meet you, too. How can I help?" Paulette perches on the chair behind her desk giving the impression that she isn't used to sitting.

"This is a lovely organization," I say, taking another sip of tea. "Such an important mission, keeping history alive. That's why I'm here today, doing a bit of research."

Paulette nods her head and maintains her attention even though her smart phone pings twice. I hurry on, intent on getting the information I came for before she gets distracted by her real work of the day.

"Josie Little Fish…she looks like someone familiar. That is, someone I'm painting. I'm an artist and am working on this piece . . ."

I fumble the sketches from my bag and hand them over the desk to Paulette. She studies them, nodding her head.

"They're lovely. The woman looks remarkably similar. Where did you get your inspiration?"

"Oh, it's . . . a long story." I take another sip of tea, hurry to ask another question. "They're both Native American; but are they from the same tribe? Can you tell me more about Josie? Or where I could get information about the natives in this area of the country?"

"Of course." Paulette is quiet for a few moments as she studies my renditions, then draws her chair closer to the middle of her desk straightening a paper punch along the way.

"How familiar are you with the history of the Champlain Valley?"

"Not very, I'm afraid. We purchased our home before I ever even visited the state. My husband, Cole, fell in love with it during his first visit. His company recently expanded and started a new location in Burlington." I pause chewing the inside of my lip. "We moved here from Philadelphia."

Paulette nods. "But that accent isn't from Philly." She smiles.

"I'm from London, originally."

"Settling in well?" She shifts in her chair, smiling again. It's warm and friendly.

"It's beautiful here, thanks."

"It takes some time to get used to. Vermont is its own little country. I've lived here my whole life, and I still feel like I don't fit in sometimes. Now, I'm not a Native historian by any means, but I do know some of the region's Native American history. The tribe in this area is Abenaki. Most people pronounce it Ab-nakee but it's actually more like AH-buh-nah-kee. The tribe was native to this area far before the French and English settlers came here. They were, or are, I should say, an agricultural people. They lived along the banks of the Missisquoi River in the old days, planting crops on the flood plains and hunting and fishing to supplement their food stores."

I interrupt.

"But you said, "are." There is still a tribe here in St. Albans?"

Paulette smiles, but it's small and sad.

"The Abenaki can still be found in Franklin County, St. Albans and beyond. They've been torn apart through the years, their tribe still unrecognized by the United States Government, even the State of Vermont for that matter. So they qualify for none of the compensation that other recognized tribes do. Convenient, some would say. Fair, others would insist.

"Swanton maintains a large population of Abenaki people. They're called the St. Francis tribe, after their once-chief, Homer St. Francis. The town is about eight miles north. I can give you the address of the Abenaki Information Center there." She pauses, reaches for a pen and writes in big, loopy script on the back of her business card. "I'm sure you'll find a lot more answers to your questions."

I thank her and follow it with another question. "But what happened to them? The people who made up the unrecognized tribe?"

Paulette shrugs, a defeated gesture.

"What happens to most Natives? Whatever it is, the Abenaki have experienced it: disease, plagues, disbursement, discrimination, even forced sterilization, though that's rarely discussed. It's a blight on the history of our great state." Paulette waves a hand around her office, the artifacts in neat piles.

"If I can offer you a word of advice, Sarah," Paulette stands from her chair and leans toward me. "Be careful what you ask and of whom, that is, if you don't enjoy conflict. Vermonters are a proud people; we think of ourselves as independent, and nothing is a better compliment to us than that we 'pulled ourselves up by our bootstraps.' But sometimes that pride hides shame, I think. In what we've done to remain independent. Who we've stepped over." Paulette glances at the large sheets of sketch paper. "Or on."

We shake hands, and I thank Paulette for her time and tuck the sketches into my bag. She gives me her card with the address for the information center on it and leads me through the winding rooms to the rear door where we say goodbye.

I shiver again as I look over my shoulder when the heavy door swings shut. I half expect to see Josie Little Fish, face pressed against the glass staring, her strange, haunted eyes wide and following me.

{Chapter Five}

It takes me fifteen minutes to drive to Swanton and another five to find the information center, which I drive past the first time. Two blocks away I nab a spot and walk. For a small town, parking is not in overabundance. I enjoy the walk, despite the cold and a light drizzle that's started. The air is crisp and cool with hints of wood smoke and pine and a less pleasant undertone of car exhaust. Two old churches flank the village green. One is red brick trimmed in white; the other small, and made of gray stone. The second boasts a magnificent stained glass window, a contemporary version of the Holy Birth.

The information center is a small, concrete building with some symbols, tribal symbols likely, painted carefully onto a large sign over the door. I don't have time to look long as the door opens, and I quickly enter, pushing damp curls out of my eyes.

The hand that opens the door is light brown, as though faded tan skin. I follow it up to the largest man I've ever seen. He is not exceptionally tall, probably just under six feet, but his girth seems nearly equal that. He's in his late thirties or early forties, with a clean shaven face and dark hair that's shaved on the sides. The rest is long and pulled back into a ponytail. His eyes are bright blue and lines around them prove he has a good sense of humor. He wears an enormous flannel green plaid shirt over baggy jeans.

"Hello." He stretches out a hand. "I'm John."

"I'm Sarah. It's a pleasure to meet you."

John cocks his head.

"You're British?"

I nod.

"Visiting?"

I shake my head. "We moved here, my husband and I, a few months ago."

"Pity," says John, walking back toward the high desk in the corner. For a minute, I think that he's insulting me until he turns back with a smile on his face. The laugh lines bunch up.

"You being married, I mean."

I laugh, and the sound surprises me. I'm rusty.

The room is warm; a small potbelly woodstove sits in the corner, the edges glowing red. In front of it is an ancient-looking hound dog, sleeping on a well-loved pillow. He snores softly, floppy lips puffing with each exhale.

"So, ma'am, what can I do for you?" John says. His hands are planted on the counter, the rest of him fills in the small space behind it.

"Wait, wait! Don't tell me. I'm going to use my sixth Indian sense and tell you what you are here for. Ready?"

I nod, still smiling.

"You were on your way to Montreal, and your car broke down."

"No, but good guess. Was it my being on foot that confused you?"

John motions with his hand for silence, closing his eyes in mock concentration. He squishes his face up, waves his hands around. I half expect him to say, "wwooooo wwooooo," but he doesn't.

"I know! This time I've got it. You're a history major and researching the Abenaki tribe in the humble town of Swanton. That it?"

I shake my head again.

"No, but you're getting closer."

I jiggle my art bag. "This is a clue."

"Hmmmm," John strokes his chin, looking carefully at the bag. "A big, black bag. You're a medicine woman? Hey, do you go by the name of Dr. Quinn?" He shrugs and smiles. "Sorry, my mojo is apparently off today. I give up."

"I'm an artist." It feels good to say the words again, as though the title somehow secures me to who I once was. "These are some sketches that I drew of someone . . ." My voice trails off. I can't very well tell him that I saw this woman in my woods. That she's a ghost.

"That is, I'm doing some research on the Abenaki tribe and I sketched someone that I thought might look the part. I was hoping you might be able to tell me if I got it right. The tribe, I mean, not the Native American part."

"Indian."

"Pardon?"

"We prefer to be called Indians."

"Oh, I'm sorry. I didn't know."

"Course you didn't. I wouldn't expect you to. I'm just telling you for future reference; you know, so you don't put your foot in your mouth."

John leans forward over the desk.

"Can I see them?"

"Of course."

I extract the sketches, and John studies them as I take in my surroundings. The place looks bigger on the inside than out. The warmth of the stove encourages me to undo the top button of my coat. The room is cozy and smells faintly of sage and strangely, rubbing alcohol. Three mismatched chairs in various stages of decline huddle near the cast iron stove, surrounding the old dog on his bed. A thick, multicolored rug which looks hand woven covers the scuffed floor just beside John's desk. The walls are blank, except for infrequent squares of wood mounted with skeletons of small mammals. A large, black and white photo peers out from the wall nearest the stove. Three women, two sitting on wood stumps and one standing, peer out from the faded picture. They're dressed in fringed skirts and simple tunics from what looks like the same material. Long, flapper-style beads hang from the eldest woman's neck and ribbons dot her hair. The trio is beautiful, dark and unsmiling.

"Yup, you got yourself an Abenkaki here." John's voice is loud in the half-empty room.

"I do?"

"Where did you say you saw her?"

"Oh, just a . . ." I fumble. "A picture in an antiques store."

John raises his eyebrows, his blue eyes looking too deeply into mine. I glance out the one small window and back again.

"My Indian mojo might be off today, Sarah, but I ain't buying that. It's okay though, you don't have to tell me."

"Does she look familiar?"

"How the hell should I know? We all look alike, right?" He laughs at this, taking any potential sting out of the question.

He waves me closer to the high desk.

"See this here?"

John points a thick finger toward the details of a band around the woman's waist. I barely remember scribbling it in.

"It's not very clear, but I can make it out. That's a wampum belt."

"Wampum?"

He nods.

"Wampum is beadwork. It's an art form, common in the Eastern woodland tribes and was actually used to record important events in a person's life. They're made out of purple and white beads which actually used to be traded as currency back in the day."

John clears his throat, his eyes looking over my face.

"You can tell a lot about an Indian's tribe and family by the design they build into the wampum. Baskets, too. They're very specific to the tribe of origin. This lady have a basket with her?"

"I don't think so. I didn't notice a basket, but I only saw her for a moment."

"Aha!" John said. "Caught you."

I blush, feeling my cheeks get as hot as the stove in the corner.

John chuckles and hands the papers back to me.

"I'd like to keep talking with you, Miss Sarah, but I'm due over to the vet's in ten minutes. Well, not me, my dog, Bailey. I try to stay away from the vet's and doctor's both. But poor ole Bailey, he's not feeling too good these days."

I gather my sketches. John motions for me to wait so we can walk out together. He walks to the elderly dog, stoops, and attaches a leash after giving a quick scratch around the neck and behind the ears. Bailey creaks to his feet, gives a little moan and then starts walking, stiff-legged, to the door.

Standing on the front step, the breeze of earlier has turned into a stiff wind. The chill of it cuts through my wool coat as though I were standing in a cotton shirt. John doesn't seem to notice. He takes his time closing and locking the door, then has to open it again to turn off the lights and relock it.

I'm shivering by the time he's finished.

"Can I give you a lift somewhere?"

"No, thank you," I manage between chatters. "I'm only a couple of blocks away."

"Hop in," John says as though I haven't spoken. He hauls the old dog into the back of the crew cab and then himself into the driver's seat of a rusted pickup. Reaching across the seat, he unlocks the passenger door and pushes it open. For a big man, he's incredibly agile.

I don't wait to be asked twice.

The truck is neat and tidy despite its outward appearance. Fast food wrappers fill a plastic grocery bag, but other than that the cab is swept clean. Even the dash looks recently dusted. It smells of old dog and spearmint and a low, clean note of aftershave.

We chat about the weather as John backs out of the driveway and retraces my path to the black

Lexus. John raises his eyebrows when I tell him to stop but doesn't say anything about the shiny car.

I smile and thank him for the ride.

"Sure, no problem. You got any other questions or want to hear more about the Abenaki, you just stop in. Here's my number, too, in case you want to call first. I don't go into the office every day; there's no need since we get so few visitors, especially this time of the year. Come Memorial Day weekend we'll have our big Pow Wow right here in the park. Maybe you could come and dance." He plows on before I can say anything. "With your husband, I mean. There are a few couple's dances we do."

I smile, imagining Cole in buckskins, dancing in a public park.

"Maybe," I say. "Thanks again." I pocket the creased card after taking a quick look. It says simply, "John Running Bear" and "Abenaki Information Center" with the phone number and street address.

Adjusting the strap of my bag I hurry to my car and slide behind the wheel, cranking up the heat dial even though it's only blowing cold air. I shiver again, hard, and rub my hands together fast, to move the blood.

John drives away with a wave and single toot of the horn. I wave back, smiling. It's been months since we've been in Vermont, and today I feel like I've finally made a friend. A lecherous one maybe, but a friend none the less.

I think about the ghost, the woman from the woods, as I maneuver the curves and dips in the road. A bright orange sign warns, "BUMP!"

seconds before my car hits a frost heave so hard my teeth snap together. I slow down, realizing how dim the light is becoming. The headlights on the car switch on as though reading my thoughts. Only a bit after six o'clock and already the grayness of the sky is pressing in, creating shadows and dimness. How do people get used to this? Not quite dinner time, and I already feel ready for a bath and bed.

I take another curve in the road and think about what John told me. The wampum is curious. I'll have to look online and see what I can learn. I feel a small glow of yellow pooling in my belly: satisfaction. It's been a long, long time since I've felt satisfaction in something I've done. It feels good.

The puddle of warmth dissipates as soon as I pull into the gated community. Marvin, the security guard that works second shift, waves me through with a head nod. I wave back, but the warmth blasting out of the heaters suddenly seems too cool. Looming shapes of bushes and houses at the end of dark driveways presses against the car windows.

It's all in your imagination. I tell myself this over and over, but nothing settles my nerves in this place. The car noses through the densely-wooded main drive, then follows a few languid curves before breaking in small patches, where driveways of pristine black pavement or pea gravel branch off. Most residences aren't visible from my car but the few that are, are stunning during the daylight. I pass one on my left, a huge white mansion, complete with pillars and stone steps. It seems to glow in the last of the evening light, as though reflecting off the dim sunlight it gathered during the day. In the summer I imagine flowers spilled out in all directions from the porch window boxes and enormous stone pillars topped with terra cotta pots. Tonight the yard is stark, though a few lights warm windows.

I look back toward the driveway, just in time to swerve and miss a squirrel. The next driveway has a mansion tucked so far back into the woods that it isn't visible. Another two are visible, though, the first, an enormous Cape Cod, barely peeping out from a cottage garden complete with arbor and flagstone patio, trees and hedge providing privacy in the rest of the yard. No lights, no movement. No life. I shiver. This time it's not from the cold.

I'm making the final winding arc before our driveway when movement on my right catches my eye. A dark shadow, darting. I slam on my brakes. A scream wrenches its way from my throat.

Standing half bent over on the side of the road is the pale figure of a man dressed completely in black. His hands hold something dark and furry. His eyes find mine in the brief second before he steps in front of my car. His lips are curled back, rimmed with blood.

{Chapter Six}

"And that's when you called us?" the police officer asks. Teeth still chattering, I nod. I'm sitting inside the cruiser, at the top of our short driveway. My heart is pounding even more loudly in the officer's car. Buttons and lights cover the dashboard, and a video camera is mounted near the windshield. The blue lights aren't flashing, and I'm grateful for that. The interior smells of stale air and faintly, cologne. I think of another cruiser, another policeman but push the thoughts away. Panic will not help me in this moment.

"Stay right here for just a minute, Mrs. Solomon. I need to talk with the other officer."

I nod my head, look toward the house.

The thought of walking into that cold crypt tonight nearly brings me to tears. As uncomfortable as I am in this car, being this close to a man in a blue uniform, part of me wants to stay here, warm and safe. I think wildly about locking the doors, burrowing myself between the seats, hands over my ears. Perhaps he'll arrest me, bring me to the county jail. At least the people there wouldn't be eating small mammals.

Live.

On the side of the road.

I shiver again and take some deep, yogic breaths. It won't help to get all worked up again. I see the two officers conversing through the side mirror.

"This one's loonier than a Canadian dollar," I picture my officer telling the other. "Thinks she saw a guy eating a chipmunk."

Was my mind playing tricks? I replay the incident again and again, trying to remember. I was so startled by the man's presence, at nearly running him down, that I saw his hands only for an instant. A small, brown body. Fluff. Blood. Or were they holding only a mitten as he said?

The driver door opens, and the young officer slides behind the wheel. His badge reads, "Chevalier." He looks at me for a few seconds, then straight ahead, draping his long hands over the wheel.

"Mrs. Solomon."

"Please, call me Sarah."

"Sarah. I've talked with Officer Perkins at length; she's talked with the ambulance driver and the man himself. He's your neighbor, by the way. The man on the side of the road. This guy's a. . ." He checks his clipboard. "Psychiatrist. You know, like a play doctor."

I smile wanly.

"Anyway, Dr. Andrew Bevins, your neighbor, he's got pneumonia. Caught it after coming back from the Bahamas last week. Change in the climate. His doctor told him it's a pretty bad case. Dr. Bevins says he was in the middle of a coughing fit when you came upon him. Too fast, he says. In fact, he said in his statement that you nearly ran him over. Is that true?"

Blood rushes to my face.

"No." I sound defensive and try again. "That is, I might have nearly hit him, but he was dressed in dark colors practically kneeling by the road. I mean, for goodness sake, who wouldn't almost run him over?"

Officer Chevalier nods. I wait for the usual questions about my driving record, any difficulty I'd experienced acclimating to driving on the opposite side of the road, on a different side of the car, but none come. He is quiet a moment, looking at his paperwork, then turns and looks at me again. His eyes are dark and serious.

"Are you on any medications?"

Blood leaves my face and hands.

"None that would interfere with my ability to drive," I respond, voice tight.

"You stated that Bevins' mouth was bloody," Chevalier moves on. "Bevins says that it was from the coughing, and that it was sputum, not blood. Are you sure of what you saw?"

I close my eyes for a minute, see him crouching, feel my hands tightening on the wheel. I open my eyes.

"No. Not sure, I guess. He was..." I gesture out the window. "He had a ring of red around his mouth. I thought it was blood. It looked like blood." My voice becomes smaller with every sentence. I feel like a complete idiot.

"Well, we didn't see anything on him when we got here, and we didn't find any small mammal with teeth marks in it." I think he wants to laugh.

I look out the window toward our gray house. Instead of welcoming and drawing me in, the windows look sinister, the stone front cold and hard. If a house could cross its arms this one was. I sigh and turn back to the officer.

"I'm sorry," I say. "It's been a really long day, and I wasn't as careful as I could have been driving. I shouldn't have even called you or made all this fuss." I wave my hand toward the other police car and the ambulance, which has turned off its lights and is slowly backing into the neighbor's driveway to turn around.

Officer Chevalier nods once, writes a last item on the report and tucks the clipboard into the holder near the passenger seat. I wonder what he's written, but he turned it so the information is pointing toward the dash.

"Dr. Bevins doesn't want to press any charges. He thinks it was an honest error in judgment and said he doesn't want any trouble. I'm not even going to give you a ticket, Mrs. Solomon. Just please, be more attentive in your driving."

I nod and exit the car when he tells me I'm free to go. Then I sit in my own car and wait until all the vehicles have left before starting it up and following the wide beams of yellow headlight all the way to the garage. It's dark out now, the sun has dropped low behind the mountains in the west.

I step out of the car, my handbag, art bag and empty coffee cup balanced precariously as I hit the button to close the overhead door. My heart nearly stops when I turn toward the street and see the figure, all in black, walking slowly past our house. A white flash of hand appears in the dark, another

swath of white below a dark, knit hat. Andrew
Bevins' face, curled into a sneer.

"Well, you're the talk of the neighborhood now,
Sarah. May I come in?"

Charlotte stands on the front steps the
following morning, bundled in a fur-lined coat and
wearing dark sunglasses though the light outdoors is
dim. She has a tray with two cups of Starbucks
balanced on opposite sides. A third hole is filled
with small packets of artificial sweetener.

I motion her inside, stepping back to allow her
room in the entry hall. I'm dressed but haven't
bothered to shower yet or put on any makeup. I
excuse myself for a minute, run upstairs and gather
my hair into a ponytail. At least the snarls won't
show. I add a little eyeliner and pinch my cheeks for
color then brush my teeth.

When I return to the living room, Charlotte is
perched precariously on the end of the cream sofa. I
sit across from her on the olive green chaise,
longing to lean back and sleep some more. Instead,
I fold the blanket from the night before and smooth
my hands over it.

"I'm sorry," I say. "Where are my manners?
Can I get you something to eat? I've made banana
bread or . . ." my voice trails when I see her
frightened-looking face. Then I remember: the low-
carb diet.

"Celery?" I ask.

"No, thank you. I'm fine. Here, coffee." She
points to one of the tall cups, and I gratefully

accept. She picks out the other and crosses her thin legs.

"So, what in the world happened last night?"

I sip my coffee, burning my tongue. It tastes terrible after peppermint toothpaste.

"Oh, it was nothing, a simple misunderstanding. I thought our neighbor, Dr. Bevins, was . . . injured."

"Really?" She asks, scooting further forward on the cushion. "He's a real piece of work, you know. Have you met him?"

I shake my head. *No, no. Unless one considers calling the authorities on a neighbor "knowing" them.*

"He's the lead psychiatrist at Jacobs-Smith. He's been there for years, worked his way up. Unfortunately, he's one of those people with a lot of money and power, but a shitty outlook on life."

Jacobs-Smith is the largest hospital in the state. I wondered why this guy's outlook was so bad. The unasked question didn't go unanswered for long.

"His wife left him a couple years ago, probably sick to death of him psychoanalyzing her every move. But he had the shitty outlook way before then. I think he was born with it." Charlotte sips her coffee.

"Out of all the people in the neighborhood, you went and pissed off Andrew Bevins." Charlotte shakes her head, sounding amazed. "He'll make your life hell." She stops, looks at me.

"Sorry. I didn't mean to scare you. He's just a…" she paused, searching the bank of windows in front of her for the right word, "a miserable person.

And his goal in life, outside of work where he always gets his way, seems to be making sure that everyone else is miserable along with him. You've heard of people who like to rain on others' parades? Well, Andrew Bevins not only wants to rain on them, he wants to torpedo them." Another sip of coffee then, "Did he say anything to you?"

I think back to last night.

"No."

"Nothing at all? Well, that's probably a good thing," Charlotte says. "He's actually pretty decent usually, or at least pretends to be, until you get on his bad side."

"Oh great. Thanks for the heads up."

She smiles.

"I wouldn't worry about it. It will blow over and everyone will forget about it."

"Everyone?"

"Sure." She looks at me as though I've sprouted an extra appendage. "Everyone in the neighborhood. Gated communities are private places which can be both good and bad. Haven't you lived in one before?"

I shake my head no.

"Ah, well. It takes a little getting used to. We're not a tight knit group, not the type that would, say, bring you soup if you're sick. But we're good at communicating and good at keeping tabs."

Great. So my neighbors are good at gossiping and checking up on each other.

"Where's your husband?" Charlotte changes the subject, looking around the room as though expecting Cole to materialize from thin air.

"What, that hasn't made the information rounds yet?" I ask, then smile hoping to take the sting out of my words. "He's out of town. He travels a lot for business."

Charlotte nods and then stands.

"Well, I have to run to Burlington, return some things. Nice chatting, Sarah."

I walk Charlotte to the door, her heels tapping loud as she walks. I thank her for the coffee and start closing the door behind her when her voice stops me.

"Sarah?"

I pause, look at her dark-colored glasses. Her eyes are just shadows behind the brown lenses.

"Be careful who you talk to around here. I mean," she pauses, looks out toward the spot where the police car was the night before. "Outsiders."

I stare at her.

"It's just that the purpose of this type of community is to live quiet, private lives. We can't do that if there are," she pauses again searching for the right word, "others here who don't belong. Just a bit of friendly advice."

She smiles brightly and waves her fingers at me. Her Louis Vuitton bumps the other hip as she balances her coffee in the same hand.

I give an anemic smile and halfhearted wave then close the door behind me.

Firmly.

{Chapter Seven}

The afternoon is spent in my art studio. I think of painting, actually open some tubes, inhaling the slightly toxic but comforting scent. Then I cap them and put them back, unused, into the cabinet. Blank canvases lean in a group on one wall. I get up and walk around the room, straightening materials, picking up stray bits of paper and tossing them in the trash, then spend long minutes staring out of the windows. The day has turned cloudy, and snow starts to fall as I stand there. Slowly the flakes twirl down, dancing from the heavens.

The next forty-five minutes are spent rearranging art magazines and books. They really need alphabetization, I reason to myself. When I next look up the gloominess outside my window is replaced with white. Fat, fast snowflakes fall so hard that I can barely make out the end of the driveway. The trees are coated, thick white as though someone layered them with gesso. I stare, mesmerized by the transformation. The quiet, at first peaceful, becomes unbearable. The only sound I can hear is the hall clock ticking. I used to enjoy the comforting sound, the happiness that I could find only in solitude. But after the Dark Time, I don't enjoy it like I used to. I shiver and move away from the windows.

I turn off the light in the studio, giving up on creativity for the day. A pot of tea sounds good, and some music. I flip on the stereo system, and the house is filled with a Mozart sonata. Feeling better after a cup of tea, I wander into the dining room, find my art bag and smooth out the sketches on the long, dark table.

The ghost stares back from the paper. I lean in for a closer inspection, but the phone rings.

I jump, then fumble with the receiver, nearly dropping it.

"Hey, darling. How are you?"

Cole's voice is warm and comforting. And far away.

"I'm fine." I force my voice to sound bright, cheerful even. "How's your trip going? Did you have the first client meeting today?"

"Yeah, it went really well. Steve thinks we've got this one in the bag. There are another two rounds tomorrow and then, if all goes well, we should be celebrating on the golf course with our newest clients enjoying the sun and sand. You should have come, Sarah."

I nod, pulling at my curls. This is a nervous habit I acquired months ago which drives Cole nuts.

"I wish I had," I say, not really wishing it at all. Business wives, that's what we're called, and I've never fit in. If one isn't interested in the latest Hollywood gossip or tearing down other business wives and getting lipo as a hobby, one doesn't gain admittance to the special club.

"I've been doing a little work," I say, hoping that Cole can't see through me on the phone. Well, it was half true. I did some sketches.

His voice is positive, upbeat.

"Wonderful, Sarah. Anything special?"

If I tell him I'm drawing ghosts, he'll worry.

"No, just some sketching. I cleaned the studio up a bit, too." Change the subject, I think.

"I met someone at the local Abenaki Information Center yesterday. I'm going to do a little research on the native population here. It's really interesting. He said I could call with any questions I have. He was very…" I want to say "normal unlike our neighbors," but don't want to start a fight, "down to earth."

"Well, that's good, darling. I'm glad you've found something to—" Cole's voice cuts out. Has the call been dropped? Then I realize he's searching for the right words.

"To focus on. New pursuits are a wonderful way to stimulate one's brain."

And keep someone from going crazy? I want to ask it but don't, pinching my tongue between my teeth, hard.

"There was a little incident here last night." I say it nonchalantly, but my heartbeat is already starting to rev up in my ears.

I fill Cole in on the disturbing run-in with the neighbor. He's quiet for a full minute.

"Hello? Still there?"

"I'm here, I'm here." Another few seconds of silence.

"Are you sure about what you saw? Maybe the guy had a bloody nose. Or it could have been the pneumonia; if he was coughing a lot that could bring up blood-tinged sputum." Cole's mother was a doctor, and sometimes his descriptions of bodily functions in medical terminology made me laugh. Not tonight, though.

"I know what I saw." I say it quietly.

"And you weren't. . ."

I let the silence hang between us for a full minute. Let him be the one to say it.

The line is crystal clear. I'm amazed I can't hear his breathing the silence is so loud.

Finally, he asks it.

"How many glasses of wine did you have?"

"None!" I say, louder than necessary.

He sighs, and I imagine his long fingers, complete with perfectly rounded nails passing over his face.

"Sarah, I know that this move hasn't been easy for you. I know you're still in the process of healing. But you make it more difficult than it has to be. You hole up in the house, don't get out to meet people."

"There's no one to meet! Our neighbors are all recluses who glare at me in the infrequent times I meet them in the car on the way in or out of the community. It's hard to get to know people who have an obvious dislike for you."

"What about this trip, then? You could have come out here, enjoyed the pool, spent some time on the greens. You isolate yourself too much, Sarah, and then you wonder why people aren't falling over themselves to spend time with you."

It's true, what he's saying, at least in part.

"I'm sorry," I say. "Maybe you're right." But even as I say it there's a small twisting in my gut. *But I'm not wrong about our neighbors. I'm not.*

Cole says something muffled to someone else in the room.

"Sorry, darling. I've gotta run. Steve and I are on our way to the course."

I picture Cole in his pressed pants and collared shirt, tanned arms and easy smile. Why can't I just be happy, content, like him?

"Sure. Call me again tomorrow?"

He agrees, and we exchange "I love you's" before hanging up.

The snow has gotten thicker outside the window, and now it blows gently against the panes of glass, swirling close, then away. I watch it for a few minutes then turn toward the kitchen. I shake one of my anxiety pills out, pour a glass of Riesling and close my eyes in appreciation. I drink the first glass too quickly and sip slowly at the second. The hard ball in my stomach is loosening.

I go back into my studio. I'm determined to do something in here: draw a stick figure, paint a circle, anything to get back into my work. But my muse, irritating thing, doesn't like to be bossed.

Instead, curling up on a wing chair in the corner of the room, I hoist one of my old sample books. It's heavy and awkward in my lap. Resting my wine glass so I won't spill, I open the portfolio.

"Sarah Solomon Designs," a bold, black typeface reminds me. "An artist and designer who makes life sparkle." I snort in derision, but tears prick my eyes. "Make Life Sparkle," that was the tagline for my newest products. Greeting cards, stationery, wrapping paper. I had even started dabbling in designing prints for fabric. I loved my work.

I think about the long days, the dark nights spent over my art table. The best thing was that it didn't feel like work to me, not most of the time. Of course, there were parts I disliked, the administrative side for one. And toward the end, the thousand and one details that went into opening a full-fledged, brick and mortar store. Cole helped a lot, though. He wasn't traveling so much for business then, and he loved all the details, the nitty gritty numbers piece that I detested. We were a good team. He built the shop's foundation, and I made it beautiful.

Flipping through the heavy pages now, the vivid colors and textures speak to me from each design. I miss making art. There is a physical ache inside, like a missing appendage. But then . . .

The wind blows hard against the house, and a tree branch too near the window taps the glass. I shiver and set down the book, pick up my almost empty glass and walk toward the door. I stop when goose bumps press against my skin. Not a warning of danger, not anxiety. I stop and walk back to my drawing table. Anticipation. I turn around and walk back to my art table, quickly.

Without thinking, I pull out the brush closest to me, two tubes of paint and the nearest canvas. My hand is trembling as I work, fast, too fast, and rough. My hand moves over the canvas, black and red paint smearing and moving and bringing me into their world. Emotions that I haven't felt in months are caught in my belly, then move to my chest and claw their way up my arms and into my hands, then finally, onto the white surface. I can't breathe, and I can't look away, and when I finish there are tears running down. Tracks of wet on every inch of my face.

I put my head in my hands, feeling paint from my fingers, wet and thick on my face, in my hair. But it doesn't matter. I stand, entranced. The first piece I've created in months, something I thought I'd never, ever be able to do again. Excitement and happiness bubble up in me, but as I look at the piece, the light dims. And then my hands start to tremble again, but this time it's not excitement or even rage or sadness but fear.

Red paint forms a rough, square shape on the canvas, thick and heavy and oppressive. There are varying shades to the crimson, though I didn't stop for gesso; the pressure of my hand and the amount of paint on the brush determined this.

It's what's in the center of the square that makes me stop breathing. A small, round opening. But this isn't frightening; it's what I've painted around the hole. A gun. 9mm. Black. The kind police carry.

I back away from the canvas.

"No." I tell the empty room.

"No. No. No."

The canvas stares back at me. Accusing. The nose of the gun point coming out of the background, taunting. I hear Billie Holiday crooning in my ear, a song I'll never forget. I smell the wet earth and feel the cold hard hands gripping me, the metal pressed against my temple. Hear the voice, rough and taunting, hot breath on my cheek.

I turn and run from the room.

{Chapter Eight}

The next morning finds me rolled into a heavy down quilt. Under that, I'm bundled with three warm layers of clothes, sitting in a rocker on the patio. I couldn't move if I wanted to. And I don't.

The light is the palest blue rising up over the horizon. I've been sitting here in the dark, watching the world come to life. My breath forms a frosty cloud, and the white of it dissipates almost immediately. Ribbons of baby pink, then soft salmon move across the eastern sky. It happens slowly, so slowly I find myself holding my breath. But then suddenly, the entire area is lit with streaks of hot pink and tangerine and crushed berries. Smears of color and brightness emanate from first one spot, then another, until rays of light fill the sky, melding the colors together like melting sherbet until they are gone.

I breathe again, inhaling the frostiness of the morning air and then finally leave my nest of blankets and return to the kitchen. I press freshly ground coffee. I squeeze oranges, and the color in my glass reminds me of the morning sky. I drink both, perched on the high stool at the granite bar, eat a toast with peanut butter.

When the food is gone, I put the dishes away and dust my hands together. Unscrewing two orange bottles from the cabinet, I take one pill from each. The first is pale blue, a tiny round dot. "This will help with the anxiety and panic," my doctor said. The second is white and oval, a magic drug that lifts the heavy cloud of depression that's followed me for months.

"It's a new day," I tell the kitchen. "I'm not going to let last night get to me. I'm not going to spend the day holed up in here, thinking about the past."

The refrigerator hums in acknowledgement, and I give the stainless beast a pat before moving to the master bedroom to remove one of the three layers of clothes. Silk long underwear are my new staple. Thin and soft, they add an extra layer of warmth without feeling like the Michelin Man. I wrestle my hair into a ponytail, tight curls fighting my fingers, then brush my teeth, and apply some lip gloss and mascara.

The plow man has just scraped our driveway and the main drive, so I climb into the car and back out slowly. On the shared road, I see our neighbor across the street putting something into her mailbox. I toot the horn in what I hope is a friendly way and wave enthusiastically. Rather than returning my wave, she stares at me in disbelief. I'm driving so slowly I'm nearly stopped, so I don't miss the hardness in her eyes or the way her lips stretch tight over her teeth. I stop mid-wave and glance at the drive, then back, but she's already walking toward her house. She doesn't turn around.

"Good morning to you, too!" I sing out in my car. Ignoring the pinch in my chest, I turn on the stereo. I crank the volume up on my favorite station, an old-time jazz that features ragtime. There aren't any other neighbors out. I wave to the day guard at the hut and then take a right, accelerating onto the main road and retracing yesterday's route to Swanton. John won't be in today, but why not go on a field trip? I can find out more about the Abenakis and see if there is any information at the historical society about the land on which our community is built.

An hour later, I give up, discouraged. The public library houses the local historical society as well, but I failed to call ahead and find out that they don't open until noon. I wander around the side streets of the town on foot, trying to kill time. I spend a little time poking around the shelves of a kitschy old-fashioned drugstore, but skip the resale baby and kids' boutique next door. The scent of fresh melted cheese and warm dough wafts out of a pizza parlor. A small diner with a large wooden fish sign, two gas stations and an antiques shop round out the businesses in the center of the town.

Walking through the village green, I stop for a few minutes to read a sign about the swans that live in the small caged area. An empty pond and a few stray feathers are all that are left. "Sam and Betty," the sign tells me, winter over in another area of the town and are expected back in early to mid-May. The town, the sign continues, may have been named after the swans, a gift from Queen Elizabeth II to commemorate the bicentennial of the town's granting. Either that or after British Naval officer William Swanton who was influential in the war against the French. I'm pulling for the Brit.

I decide to head back to the car when I spot a sign that mentions Abenaki. I read it. "Historic landmark of the Abenaki tribe can be found at the end of Monument Road, off of Spring Street." I glance at the road sign above me which is the same.

Perfect. I retrace my steps to my car and pump up the heat while following the minimal directions. Sure enough, driving about a mile and a half north on Spring Street leads to Monument Road, on the left. I make the turn and follow the dirt road another two miles. There are small, well-kept homes along the road in batches, with space between for a large swamp and lots of woods.

The road is potholed, and I make the mistake of going too fast initially. A few minutes later, taking a final curve and following a river, I see several more houses, and then the road dead ends. A white Cape Cod house stands directly opposite from a large stone monument, shrouded in shrubbery. I park near the small island of trees and stone and get out.

Walking to the monument, I first notice colorful threads and ribbons, some rolled into tight bundles, others perhaps that have been teased by the wind, dancing on the bare branches. The river, brown and fast, rushes past, down a steep bank. I imagine falling in, shiver at the thought.

I look again at the large stone. The monument stands about six feet high and maybe three feet wide. The inscription is worn away, too hard to read. But a small sign, about knee-level, stands nearby. It talks about various animals special to the Abenaki people: turtle, otter, wolf, beaver, bear and eagle. The description leads me to believe a totem pole once stood near the monument.

"What are you doing?"

A gruff voice startles me. I turn quickly to see a flannel-shirted man, belly protruding, and greasy ball cap covering hair in need of a trim. He's in his late fifties and doesn't look friendly.

"I'm, uh…" I stumble on my words, collecting my thoughts. Then heat fills my middle, and I draw up to my full height, pull my shoulders back.

"Do you own this monument? I was under the impression it was public property." I look directly into his eyes, which are lined with heavy wrinkles. First rule of backing down a bully: direct eye contact.

"Nah, I don't own it. But I do watch over it. Live over there," he nods toward a green trailer which is surprisingly neat and tidy compared to its owner.

"Well, I appreciate your concern in doing your civic duty, but I'm just reading the inscription. I'm doing a bit of research, and John at the Abenaki Information Center told me that I might want to see this." I turn my back on him. I'm a terrible liar.

"That right?" The man's voice has changed. I turn back.

"Paul Gregoire." He sticks out a hand. It's hard and full of calluses, but he smiles so warmly I barely notice.

"Sarah. Sarah Solomon," I say after a slight pause.

"Sorry about giving ya the third degree. We've had problems with vandalism here, racial slurs on the stone and removal of some of the bags." He points a thick finger at the brightly twined bundles in the tree branches around the monument.

"They're dream bundles for the next life. Abenaki stuff, you know."

"Are you? Abenaki, I mean."

"No, uh-uh." Paul pulls out a pack of Marlboros which look like they've lived in his pocket for the past decade. "Trying to quit," he apologizes, then offers me one. I shake my head as he lights his.

"Nope. I'm no Abenaki, but I'm friends with a few. John, he's a good man. A handful of others too, most of 'em fishing buddies, most of 'em only part. It's rare to find full-blooded Indians these days in Vermont. The eugenics project in the 30s and then the smallpox epidemics before that wiped a lot of them out."

A curl has escaped the ponytail holder and blows across my nose. I stick it behind my ear.

"What's the eugenics project?"

Paul takes a deep drag, holding the smoke in his lungs for a long minute before turning to look at the river to our left and letting it trail out of his lips.

"Not from around here, are you?" He chuckles, a deep ragged sound. His lungs sound full and wet. "Guess I should've known from that accent."

I smile, hoping to keep the story going.

"From London, originally."

Paul nods.

"Huh," is his only reply. "Well, the eugenics study in a nutshell," he pauses, takes another drag. "It was an attempt by the state to wipe out the "undesirables" from this fine land. You know, Vermonters are a proud people; they'll tell you that if you can't trace your family line back seven generations here, you're not a true Vermonter. Funny thing is that the Abenaki trace their lines back thousands of years, but the state still don't recognize them as a tribe. Would have to help 'em out then, and they don't want to do that. That eugenics project wasn't just for natives, though. Our state weren't too keen on French Canadians or Jews or Italians, or the mentally ill, either. Pretty much anyone who wasn't English-born wasn't wanted. Think of it like Vermont's version of the Holocaust."

Paul stops for another drag, and I wait.

"What was done to them?" I'm suddenly conscious of my own English accent.

"Oh, they were placed in boarding schools, hospitals. Some of them were even put in the mental institution in Waterbury. They were "fixed" if you know what I mean. All in the name of science of course, studying 'em and all that, but mostly the point was to sterilize 'em. Make sure they couldn't make more generations of mutants. Just like the Germans did."

My stomach pinches. I wait another moment while Paul stubs his cigarette out on the gravel nearby and then tucks into his pocket.

"Disrespectful to litter," he mumbles, then looks again toward the river.

"Well, Sarah, I got to get back to a carburetor that's just dead set on staying broke. It was nice chattin' with you."

"Thank you for taking the time," I say. I point to my camera in the leather bag on my hip. "Is it okay to photograph the monument?"

"Don't see why not," Paul says. He puts his fingers to his cap lightly and then turns toward his trailer. "Tell John I said hello next time you see him."

I take my time with the photos, getting in as close as I can without cutting off text from the monument. A few close-up shots of the dream bags, and I'm done. I stand for a few more minutes, though. The quiet spot is restful. The sun peeks across the far meadow and warms my face, and instinctively I turn toward it, like a cat. The river is loud and moves fast high up on the banks. Spring runoff.

Minutes later, I retrace my footsteps to the car and climb in, moving the camera to the passenger seat and checking the clock. John may be in the office now. I start the car and head back toward the center of the village.

He's not there. A sign on the door indicates that he was, but stepped out for an unplanned appointment. The office won't be open again until Thursday. Two more days. I sigh and get back into the car, then head south on Route 7 toward home.

{Chapter Nine}

The house is unlocked when I arrive. A giddy rush of excitement runs through me. Cole is home from his trip two days early. I leave the Lexus sitting in the driveway; later I'll go out for a few groceries. I nearly skip into the house. I've missed him. And, I realize unexpectedly, I've felt really lonely. The prospect of enjoying hours of companionable conversation sounds so much better than the forecast my evening held previously: wine, a half-hearted attempt at supper and avoiding my studio. With maybe a little mindless television thrown in for good measure.

It's cold inside; I notice this first. So cold that I'm surprised my breath isn't coming out in white puffs. I stand, rubbing my gloved hands up and down my arms as I walk through the rooms one by one. Lights aren't turned on; weird shadows play in corners.

"Cole?" Several seconds of silence, then I hear a noise to my left coming from the great room. I move in that direction. My stomach knots itself, and my breath becomes shallow.

"Cole? Is that you?" Pause. "Everything okay?" My voice bounces off the large paintings and the hall console and the glass chandelier. My footsteps seem incredibly slow in the hallway, walking suddenly an effort.

I place my hand on the pocket doors. *Had I closed them before I left this morning?* The sound comes again from the other side of the doors, scratching, like branches against a stone wall or something dry and light moving across something else. My heartbeat fills my ears. My hands, ice cold, slowly push the doors apart. Is the sound becoming louder? The blood in my ears is pounding hard, and I can't tell. My knees are shaking, and there is a familiar smell that I can't place but which shouldn't be here, in this room.

The doors open slowly, and I feel like I'm on a carousel. The room expands and then immediately contracts. At first glance, the room appears the length of a football field, but in the next breath, shrinks so that I can see only the thing across the room. The thing that is scratching gently against the wall.

My hands are over my mouth, trying and failing to keep in a scream. The wall on the far side of the great room, pale gray and softly lit by a single table lamp, is pierced through its middle. A knife, running with blood, shoots straight and hard out of the plaster. It holds two things beneath its blade: my painting, the one I made last night that scared me so badly, and something small and white, waving and moving in the breeze.

It takes several minutes before I come to my senses. Even longer before I can force the dead weights on the end of my legs to move toward the thing. My breath comes in jerky fits and starts, the room undulating like angry waves around me.

Finally, finally I reach the wall. My hand automatically clasps the handle of the knife, pulling it out fast and hard. Bits of sheetrock fall like crumbs onto the Oriental carpet. I stare, zombie-like at the blade, shimmering silver with red, gummy residue. Not blood, paint. Partially dried. The smell of it, oily and thick, fills the space. The knife drops to the floor, narrowly missing my foot. The painting slides down the wall and collapses onto itself, but it's the small, postcard-sized paper stuck with the knife that I reach for. My fingers, still shrouded in gloves, lift the paper up off the floor.

Three words.

Do you remember?

For a terrible moment, I think I'm going to vomit. Acid and nerves are swirling my leftover lunch. I hold a hand to the chair nearest me. *Breathe. Breathe.*

Who did this? That thought is drowned out by another, louder and more persistent. Is whoever did this still in the house? The frigid air in the room brings me out of my stupor, and I suck in great swallows of it. Looking up to the right, the wide floor-to-ceiling window is open. The glass moves back and forth, tree branches tapping it as it moves toward them then silencing as the wind blows it nearer the house. I move to it without conscious effort, the paper still clenched between frozen fingers. *Do you remember?* Mechanically, I close the window.

Thirty minutes later, Officer Chevalier is sitting in the great room with me, a pot of orange tea between us. I'm on my third cup while he has yet to take a sip.

"And you didn't notice if anything looked out of place when you arrived?" All his questions are asked in the unemotional way that professionals use when they don't want to sway your opinion. Or maybe when they are bored at the end of a long day.

I shake my head no.

"What time did you arrive?"

I have no idea where the day has gone or even what time it is now. Afternoon? Morning? I glance toward the windows. The light is just turning the palest shade of purple in the western sky.

Calculating quickly, my voice responds, "Between three and four o'clock, I think."

"And where were you coming from?"

"Swanton."

His eyebrows raise, but he says nothing, only finally takes a very small sip of tea.

"Doing what, if you don't mind my asking?"

I have the feeling this isn't really a question, just a polite way of getting the information he needs.

I give him a condensed version of my trip. He nods and writes something on his paper.

"Do you know anyone who dislikes you intensely?"

The change in his line of questioning throws me momentarily off balance.

"You mean, like an enemy?"

Officer Chevalier shrugs, then nods.

"Anyone in the area you've maybe had a run-in with, someone perhaps that you had a bad business deal with or any..." he pauses, looking embarrassed, "personal problems that have come up recently? Family issues? Your marriage?"

"No, none. Well," I stop, correcting myself, "only with Dr. Bevins, the neighbor from the other night. But I can't imagine he'd break into our home." The officer watches me over his clipboard but says nothing.

"Why would anyone do," I motion toward the painting and the hole, "that?"

"I don't know, ma'am, but I'm going to do my best to find out."

Chevalier straightens his shoulders which had drooped slightly forward. I wonder if his mother has often corrected his posture or if he's trying to make himself feel more confident. He's so young, barely old enough to legally purchase a handgun, I think.

He nods toward the hole and a second officer taking photos of it. Chevalier stands, careful to put his chair back in precisely the same spot that it occupied before. Together we walk toward the wall. The painting, my painting, is now face up, an ugly, jagged gouge in the middle. The paper looks like I feel: torn open, vulnerable.

"Can you tell me about this piece?" He stares down at it, cocking his head slightly to one side then another.

"It's something I just did the other night, completely out of character for me."

"Out of character how?"

"Well, I don't normally paint weapons; even the strokes and methods are quite unlike my work. Do you know anything about art?"

"A little," Chevalier shrugs then takes a quick look at the other, older officer photographing the area.

"I'm a mixed media artist. It's a fancy term for using more than one application method in a single piece of work. For instance, I might paint with oil or acrylic, then use inks to write verses into the canvas, then add paper pieces or found objects. Though I usually add those to my assemblage pieces."

"Assemblage?"

The officer's initial hesitation has disappeared, and he's looking between me and the painting like a tennis game spectator.

"It's a form of art where you create a sort of three-dimensional collage. I use found objects a lot, what other people might consider refuse. Working with things that have been discarded, finding their natural beauty. It's fascinating."

Consciously, I stop myself. The police don't need my artist statement or curriculum vitae to help figure out who's responsible for this. I take a big, slow breath.

"But this painting, the one here, it's yours." It's a statement, not a question.

I nod.

"It is."

Please, don't ask me to tell you what it means.

"Can you tell me what it means?"

I expel the large breath and shake my head.

"Not really. Something from a long time ago, but it has nothing to do with this situation."

I'm prepared for further questions, pressing me to share information that has stayed locked away for many months. But none come.

Chevalier nods, looks toward the window where the other officer is photographing the latch and the area in and around the casing.

"Windows locked?"

"Pardon?"

"Windows. You keep them locked?"

"Yes, of course."

"Home security system?"

"No. We didn't think it was necessary seeing as it's a gated community."

Chevalier looks at me, assessing.

He's formulating a question, I can tell. I wait, knot in stomach.

"There's no sign of forced entry."

Pause.

"Really?"

"No, ma'am. There are also no footprints outside the window." Chevalier looks away from me, shifts his weight. "The fingerprint kit may tell us something, but that's only if gloves weren't used."

His insinuation hits hard. He didn't say, "The intruder didn't use gloves," but rather, "Gloves weren't used."

"Wait a minute. Do you think I did this?" I wave my hand toward the painting, the blemished wall.

Chevalier simply looks back at me.

"Why would I do that? And why would I call you?"

"We don't know anything yet, Mrs. Solomon. I'm just giving you some of the facts as I see them."

I excuse myself, go to the kitchen. I wipe a counter that doesn't need it, straighten my cookbooks, and then catch a reflection of myself in the glass over the sink. My hair is wild, curls tangled. My eyes are wide, an expression I've seen before: panic. *Don't freak out. Do not freak out.*

"We're just about done here." Chevalier walks into the kitchen moments later. "I'd like to take a walk around the house, just to make sure there's nothing else out of order."

Code for making sure that there isn't someone in the house that shouldn't be. Or maybe, in light of our conversation, to make sure I haven't done any other crazy and destructive things elsewhere that need to be photographed and noted in his report. I nod, grateful despite my anger.

Half an hour later, both officers are heading toward the door, paperwork in hand. I get their coats from the hall closet and show them out. Chevalier promises to get in touch the moment they have any information. He says this with an unreadable expression. Part of me wants to grab his arm and plead with him to believe I didn't do this. Instead, I nod and thank them for their time.

I pass on the wine tonight, filling a tumbler with bourbon three times and taking an extra one of my special relaxing pills before calling Cole. I get his voicemail and leave a message asking him to call me when he has a chance. I hope that my voice doesn't give me away.

{Chapter Ten}

The next morning I am determined to patch the wall and remove evidence of what happened in my home. If I can't see it, it didn't really happen, right? A sheetrock repair kit at the hardware store comes first, then sanding and vacuuming. The putty knife fills the gaping hole, then another round with the vacuum. The knife found in the wall wasn't taken in as evidence as I expected. Since it was one of ours, it was returned to the kitchen after fingerprinting and now sits in the dishwasher.

Repairing the wall felt good, and I wander through the house, peeking into rarely used rooms, looking for another project that needs tackling. Everything is tidy, though, perfect furniture groupings in perfectly proportioned rooms with nothing out of place. I run the vacuum anyway and dust every room in the house.

I'm working in the last room, running the duster over smooth surfaces. The space has remained largely untouched since we moved in. A collection of boxes that have yet to be opened, mostly old work records of Cole's are stacked along one wall. One of the large cardboard containers holds trophies from his fencing days; he was quite good in his prime. In fact, he had his hopes pinned on the Olympics when a knee injury shattered his chances.

The boxes line the white wall neatly, like a perfect row of stacked wood. The rest of the room holds an accumulation of extra furniture that we plan to use in the house someday. There are always a few stray pieces during the moving process that just don't fit into the layout. It's usually not until they've been sold or donated that the perfect spot opens for them.

My forehead is damp, arms feeling tired as I finish dusting the baseboards and notice the closet door. A small cobweb hangs suspended between it and the wooden trim around the wall near the window. Have I even opened that door since we moved in? Whisking the cobweb away, I turn the handle on the door.

The space is long and narrow, a few dust bunnies the only inhabitants. I retreat back into the spare room and retrieve the vacuum cleaner. The noise is loud in the small area. The machine roars and nips at the carpet, leaving fresh streaks of darker colored carpet and the smell of dust and heat. I'm about to close the door when I notice the recessed trap door in the corner ceiling, a perfect square of about three feet all around. The attic access. I've never been up there, though Cole climbed up with the house inspector. He told me later that all looked well.

Curiosity piques, and I haul a ladder from another room which has been prepped with primer but not painted yet. I position it under the opening. Pushing up on the square door, my arms strain. Nothing. I rearrange myself at what I hope is a better angle and push again. Hard. This time the door moves upward just a little, with a creak. I brace myself against the wall behind me and push harder still. My face is hot, and I feel the throb of my pulse in my forehead. *There.* It opens.

I climb up one step, then two, pushing my hands flat against the door until I am up far enough to shove it out of the way. It smells like wood and dust motes and the staleness that all enclosed spaces have. There is no electricity, but a large window spans most of the length of the attic on the far side of the room. I have vague recollections of Cole saying it would be a great bonus room. It's chilly, and in the half-light from the window it's hard to see. I squint, trying to make out the floor space.

Wide wooden beams run the length of the room, lined between with puffy strips of pink insulation. A hammer leans against one wall, old and chipped. A few stray pieces of lumber, small leftovers, are scattered about under the window. Cobwebs line the corners, but other than that the area is empty. I rub my hands fast up and down my arms and move to retrace my steps.

It's when I've placed my right foot on the top step that I see it. Hanging from the ceiling, a slight movement catches my attention first: a sway. I put my hand up toward it, almost unconsciously, but the light from the window is gray and flat. I can't make out the details, only the shape. A bag? Or maybe a piece of fabric gathered together. It's transparent, pink or red. The material is see-through but there is something inside. Something pressing against the sides, making the small sack bulge.

What in the world. . .

I hurry down the ladder, my fingers registering the warmer climate immediately. Grabbing a torch from the hall closet my feet pound back to the storage room, climbing the ladder fast. My hand shakes, making the light bounce around the surface of the wall. I stare at the bag. A mulberry-colored mesh sack. But what's inside stops my breath in my chest for a moment. A wave of dizziness rolls over me, and for a second, I think that I'm going to fall and tumble backward down the ladder, like the Weeble-Wobble I had as a child, falling end over end. I take in great gulps of air. The sound of my breathing fills the large space, echoes off the cold walls. Then I stop, hands frozen, pulse throbbing hard in my neck.

"This can't be." My voice is a coarse whisper that I barely recognize.

The bag, swinging gently on an unseen nail, is filled with something dark. Something familiar to me but so out of place that my mind can't quite catch up.

Hair. A small mound of what looks like brown human hair, tangled in a pink mesh bag. I stare, unbelieving.

What is it doing here? In this house? This room? The questions knot in my brain. I crouch back, sitting on my feet, mesmerized by this little piece of horror in my home. The torch matches my breath, erratic and wobbly.

I close my eyes, instantly remembering the ring of blood around Dr. Bevins' mouth, his teeth pulled back in a snarl. Wolf-like. I think of the other neighbors, the cold glances and icy looks. "The purpose of this type of community is to live quiet, private lives," Charlotte had said. What type of privacy was she talking about? And what kind of community?

I shudder and scramble back across the boards to the ladder. Pulling the attic door down behind me with more force than necessary, I nearly slide back down the ladder. My heartbeat is loud but my breath is louder. I prop the ladder against the wall and slam the closet door closed. For good measure, a tall stack of boxes is pushed and shoved against the door, then the ladder against those.

My hands fumble with a glass of wine in the kitchen even though it's not yet noon. I pace the floor, willing my nerves to calm themselves, for my breath and heartbeat to slow.

Fifteen minutes later, I've calmed down enough to check my cell phone. Cole hasn't left any messages. He's due in tonight though, and I welcome the thought. He'll have an answer, I'm sure. A completely sane, reasonable answer.

I can't stay in this house. I drive too-fast on curved rural roads to Grace's Place, a small, one-woman bakery across from the village green. The village brown is a more apt description now. People meander along the sidewalks zig-zagging the town. Some are bundled in brightly-colored coats—fuchsia, robin's egg blue, sunflower yellow—snubbing their noses at Mother Nature and her leftover snow storms and bleak outlook. Older people sport woolen toques and muck boots; the younger generation wear sleek dark jackets and high leather boots, heads bare. The park in the center of town is soggy, the single fountain lined with ice and dirty snow.

I push the bakery door open, sleigh bells on a wide strap announcing my arrival. My hands are trembling, but the bakery is warm and inviting with the scent of warm butter, sugar and the dark, sharp undertones of freshly ground coffee. Peacock-colored walls showcase artwork by Vermont artists all crammed together in a mishmash fashion that gives the café an eclectic, funky feel.

Grace is a short, plump woman with a homely, kind face. Like a bar tender or a hair stylist, she is a great listener, and I suspect that I'm not the only person who comes here as much for her listening skills as the delicious food. She's working behind the counter now, rearranging half-full trays into full ones and glances up, smiling. I smile in return, but it's watery, anemic. A red swinging door separates the space behind the counter from the kitchen, which she goes through now, empty trays resting on her shoulder.

The floor plan is simple. Bakery cases line two walls toward the back of the space with tall blackboards behind filled with a carefully written out menu. The blackboards, she told me once, were saved from an 1800s one-room schoolhouse in St. Albans Bay.

"I'll be right with you," Grace says, coming from the kitchen with a tray filled with something brown and gooey and delicious looking.

"No hurry," I say and glance around.

Three customers in their mid-twenties sit at a single round table nearest the windows talking and laughing, Grace's famous Bakery Plate between them. It features all of Grace's most popular treats in miniature form. Tiny croissants filled with chocolate and local raspberry preserves, buttery maple shortbread, cheese-filled blintzes and single-bite éclairs filled with cream or custard. This group has made its way through most of the plate, crumbs and sticky fingers evidence.

The rest of the tables, mismatched and topped with clean vintage tablecloths, stand empty. The bakery, a sign above the register says, closes at four. I've been before in the early morning after bringing Cole to the airport, and crowds filled the tables to overflowing. Once there was a line backed up to the sidewalk. Sleepy-eyed commuters waited for the first cup of the day then, while exhausted mothers of early-rising toddlers bought muffins and chocolate milk and wondered how they'd have enough patience to make it through the long hours until naptime.

Bright, chaotic artwork lining every inch of the walls. Does she change the pieces out constantly? Every time I'm here I see new works. Today a turquoise cow, drawn in a messy, abstract fashion, mesmerizes me. She's chewing a mouthful of daisies in a purple field. The paint strokes are thick and uneven, making me want to put fingertips to the canvas and feel the texture.

"That's a great one, isn't it?"

I jump, purse falling from my shoulder onto the floor.

"Sorry," Grace says. "Didn't mean to startle you. Is everything alright?"

I stoop to retrieve my purse.

"Of course, silly of me. I was just deep in thought."

She nods, but her brown eyes look my face over carefully.

"You sure? You look very . . . white."

"Whiter than usual? I must be nearly transparent." I laugh, but it sounds creaky and forced. Which it is.

"It's my good English bloodlines, I suppose. The sun is not a friend."

Grace smiles then, and her plain face is transformed for an instant into beauty.

"Come, sit down with me. I was just going to have my afternoon coffee and croissant. What can I get you?"

I follow her to the bakery cases. Our feet cause the old oak floors, marred and honey-colored, to squeak. The cases are half full since it's nearly closing time, but there is still a good selection. Grace donates the leftovers each day to the area nursing homes, she told me once, and takes turns between them so no one gets hurt feelings.

Half of a six-layer chocolate cake stands near a platter of maple bars topped with a walnut and oatmeal crumb. Rhubarb pie laced with delicate pastry lattice, two plates of scones, and a dish of caramel studded cookies fill out the case. I choose a blueberry scone with a soufflé of maple yogurt on the side for dipping and a mug of coffee. We move to a booth covered with leopard print vinyl near the counter, both of us scooting as close to the wall as possible.

Large overhead fans suspended from a tin ceiling push the warm air back into the space. I nearly groan when I take the first bite of my scone.

The blueberries taste fresh and explode against my tongue. The soufflé is as airy and whipped as meringue. The dark roast coffee balances it perfectly, rich and hot and acidic.

"Delicious, Grace. You have a gift," I say around a third bite of scone.

Grace smiles, dips her head. We take turns sipping our drinks, and then she asks, "You're sure you're okay?"

Except for John Running Bear, Grace has been the single friendliest person I've met since coming to Vermont. Other than Charlotte, of course. But Grace is different. Genuine. Kind. I don't feel the need to walk on eggshells around her as I do Charlotte. I can just be myself. If only I knew who that was.

The events from the past few days disappear for a few minutes in this cozy, colorful place that smells of comfort. In an instant, though, it all comes rushing back and then the tears come, filling my eyes and running over my cheeks. I grab paper napkins, embarrassed beyond belief. The English don't cry in public, rarely even in private. "Unseemly," my grandmother would say, "Undignified."

I feel the warmth of fingers pressing on my hand.

"Hey, Sarah. It's OK. Everything is going to be fine."

This makes the tears come faster. I want to talk to her, to assure her that it's nothing serious, but I can't. I don't trust my voice to do anything but howl at this point. I say nothing. Grace sits quietly, her hand holding mine, giving it a gentle squeeze every few seconds. French music drifts out of the kitchen. It's the only noise besides my mewling into the scratchy napkins.

"I'm so sorry." I wipe away the last tears, dab at my nose. "I don't know what came over me." The group of twenty-somethings are packing up, adding dirty dishes to the pink bin that sits near the garbage can, winding scarves around their necks. They wave to Grace as they depart, and she calls after them to have a wonderful evening, thanking them for stopping in.

She turns to me then, her brown eyes warm, face inviting.

"Tell me," she says.

And I do.

I tell her about the ghostly woman in the woods, about the unnerving hollowness of the new house, the strange coldness of the neighbors, the knife and note, and the most recent discovery this afternoon. She nods, sipping her coffee and murmuring encouraging sounds every so often. Finally, I tell her about Dr. Bevins and the horrible incident in the driveway.

When I finish, my hands have stopped shaking and a great weight has lifted from my chest. My shoulders resume their natural position; I hadn't realized how high they'd risen and wonder for a moment how long they've been that way.

"Sarah, I want to tell you something about the Hawthorne Estate and about your neighbors, but I don't know quite how to say it." Grace gives my hand another squeeze, then withdraws it. She stares out the window to our right.

"Please do," I say. And I mean it. Whatever it is can't possibly be worse than what I'm fearing right now.

Can it?

{Chapter Eleven}

"I'm not sure of any details," Grace says, then sips her mug of coffee. It's strong and black and the smell of it in this moment makes my stomach roil. I push away the rest of the scone.

"I hear a lot of things here. Can't help it. It comes with the job, I guess," Grace pauses, looks past me toward the door as though envisioning the lines that form in the early morning. "And it's good in a way. I'm a believer, a Christian. And when I hear all these stories of tragedy and secret pains, it gives me something to pray about. Gives people someone to pray for them. Sometimes right here in the cafe with the person who is going through it."

My fingers are trembling slightly. I still them by pressing them flat onto the top of the table. If Grace notices, she doesn't say anything.

"But often, too often, I hear things second or third hand," she continues. "It's an old farming community and most of my customers are third, fourth or even fifth generation. Everybody knows everybody else. Sometimes that's a good thing and sometimes," she pauses, blows air out of her cheeks, "not so much."

My stomach is clenched, and I want to scream out, "What? What is it you know?" Instead, I take a small sip of my coffee. I worry that I won't be able to swallow it, that I'll begin choking and gasping right here in front of her. But the warm liquid goes down, and I nod.

"There's been talk for some time that the fortress," she pauses, looks chagrined. "That's what

the locals call Hawthorne Estates, 'The Fortress.'
Well, people have told me that it's, well, not right.
Things going on that aren't exactly kosher."

"How so?"

Grace squirms in her seat and then looks at me
directly. Her brown eyes are soft and warm, like
melted chocolate.

"Like unholy. Unnatural. Not of this world."

I sit back in my seat, still staring into her face,
trying to keep her centered in a world that feels like
it's moving around me.

"You mean like witchcraft or black magic or
something? Werewolves?" I chuckle at this last bit,
but it's forced.

She nods at first, but that's followed quickly by
a headshake.

"No. No werewolves, but maybe witchcraft or
something even darker. There have been a lot of
strange stories, things people have heard or seen on
the back side of the hill that's given them the creeps.
Weird things that can't be explained away by a
certain slant of light or time of day." She pauses.
"Some people say that there are Satanists living
there."

My brain, sluggish until now, begins to turn
with more fluidity. *Satanists. . .*

"Are you sure it isn't just a case of localism? I
mean, the native Vermonters here and the people
who live in the community aren't exactly in the
same . . ." I stop, realizing how this sounds.

"Social bracket?" Grace responds without
anger.

I shake my head. "I was going to say that we're outsiders," I say, "but yes, we are in a different social bracket as well, I suppose."

"Could be," she says then takes a bite of her pastry. She chews for a few moments in the relative quiet of the bakery. The whir of industrial fans fills the space between us.

"It could very well be what you said," Grace says, "or it could be something else. I'm only telling you what I've heard in hopes that it might help you. If you didn't live there, if you hadn't told me all this," she waves her hand in the air as though my words still float there, "I wouldn't have said a word. It's not up to me to start rumors or," she pauses, "to continue them."

"Thank you." I give her hand a quick squeeze then replace it on my mug, now cool. "For your honesty. I know this isn't the sort of thing that you believe in."

"Why do you say that?"

"Because of your faith. This must all seem rather," I pause, "silly to you."

"Evil is evil, Sarah. It's been present since the beginning of time and will continue right up till the end of it. Ghosts? Goblins? Not sure I believe in those, but I believe in darkness and evil. And spirits, good and bad. And I believe that there may be some up there." Grace looks out the window, east, in the direction of my cold gray house on a cold wintry street.

I shiver and nod, glance at the clock. It's nearing four, almost time for Grace to close up. I wish suddenly that there was somewhere else I had to go. Maybe I could go to the market, get a few things for dinner. And the florist for a fresh bouquet. The thought cheers me. I try to pay for my scone and drink, but Grace waves me away.

"Stop in again, anytime. And not just to eat or drink. Really," Grace gives me a half-hug as she walks me across the creaking wood floor to the door with the sleigh bells. "Anytime, Sarah."

"Thanks. I will." I say.

And I mean it.

"That's right, because I'm crazy!" I slam the door to the bedroom, then slide down it and into a heap on the floor. The sentence finishes my conversation-turned-argument-turned-screaming-fight with Cole. He's been home from the airport less than three hours, and already we've showered, made love, eaten and fought miserably.

The red clock digits remind me that it's nearly midnight. I'm so tired, physically, mentally, emotionally. But now, adrenaline coursing through my veins, I know I won't be able to sleep. For one insane moment I consider bundling up and walking in the woods. Anything to be out of this house. This crazy, stupid, evil house.

"It's wrecking us. Me!" I had yelled at him. "I hate it here. There's a bag of human hair in the attic, for pity's sake, Cole. Hair! Do you think I'm imagining that?"

Cole had been quiet, still processing the details I'd poured over his head like ice water. The last few days seemed like months, and I'd felt more and more insane. In Cole's defense, it was a lot to take

88

in during the short hours since he returned home. But I couldn't hold it in anymore. I was a volcano, an information volcano.

He'd moved, tiredly, into the spare room, up the ladder and into the attic. Retrieved the bag with gloved hands and a grimace, then showed me its contents. A bat. Dead, for some time it seemed. Its tiny brown wings paper thin, were pocked with holes. Its eyes missing, body shriveled, furry belly pressed against the pink mesh.

"It's a bat, Sarah. That's all. I'll take care of it."

Worry and concern had shaded his eyes, then something I recognized and remembered all too well from our time together months earlier. From the Dark Time.

Disbelief.

He didn't have to say a word, though when he did, my fear had become reality. I knew what he was going to say before the words fell from between his lips. He'd rubbed a hand over his face. Tired. Sad.

"Are you sure it's this place? This house that's the problem? You've been so isolated here, Sarah. Too much time on your hands. I wish you'd have come with me on this last trip. It would be good for you to get away."

"Am I sure?" I'd fired the words back. "Am I sure that I saw these things? Are you seriously asking me if I imagined them? Or, no wait, I know!" I said, sarcasm burning the edges of my tongue. "Sure I'm not nuts? Haven't fallen off the deep end again? Needing to go back to the loony bin, maybe?"

Cole had looked at me one long moment before passing a hand over his face. His fingers were beautiful, long and tan. He'd pinched the bridge of his nose, eyes closed. I'd wished for a moment I could take back the words, but there was a hard place in my chest that glowed with satisfaction.

There was silence for several moments, and it might have been the end of the argument if I'd let the embers rest. But I didn't. All the anger and frustration and fear I'd felt in the last few days had come pouring out. And that is how I end up behind the closed door in our bedroom, sitting in the dark, watching the numbers on the clock change.

We didn't used to fight like this. Sunny days between us were the norm ironically, when we lived in rainy, overcast England. We had loved to tour the countryside on the weekend, finding pubs and tea houses, antique shops and art galleries tucked in out-of-the-way places. We used to drive long distances, park the car along a village street and walk a radius of many miles to find the best the place had to offer.

Cole, unlike most Americans I'd met, enjoyed traditional English food. After all that walking in the fresh air, our indulgence in fish and chips or beef and hash and pints of dark, foamy beer would be well-deserved. We'd enjoy our food and talk for hours, listening to the musical cadence of voices in the background, the loud football matches on TV and the louder group gathered around offering criticism to Manchester United or Aresenal players.

Even moving to America hadn't brought with it the normal stress and fighting that one would expect. We were very, I don't know, easy people. We got on well because we enjoyed the same things, for the most part. We enjoyed each other most of all. If the other person wanted something badly, it was a joy to give it to them, not a drudgery like so many married couples made it out to be.

But not now. In this house there have been few sunny days.

Sleep won't come easy tonight, but there is nothing to be done for it. Except . . . I move to my art room down the hall, pull open the mini fridge. Bottles stand in neat rows. I help myself to a small bottle of Merlot, find a slim orange bottle of meds tucked between paints in the drawer near my drawing table. Vicodin. *Just to take the edge off.*

I sit on the high stool at the work table. The markers are lined in perfect rows. The bottles of paint sit on the shelf nearby, arranged in the order of the color wheel. Brushes are clean and stand at attention in an old canning jar. My edges are beginning to blur as I sip from a second small bottle and rub my free hand over my face.

How did I get here? To this place where what I love to do most, where the person I care most about, are both so foreign to me?

{Chapter Twelve}

Sun winds its fingers through the curtains to find my face. My response is a moan. It takes thirty minutes until I'm awake enough to stagger into the bathroom off of our bedroom. I stare at my reflection in the mirror. It might make me laugh, on a different day. My curly hair twists wildly around my head, dark smudges under my eyes look like bruises, and my cheeks are so white the freckles stand out ridiculously. My teeth feel coated and my tongue thick.

Cole has already left for work. I heard him moving around earlier. Steam fills the room while I shower, feeling the dull achiness in my head loosen, then slip down the drain. *Today is a new day.* I tell myself this several times as I'm toweling off and applying makeup. *A new day and a fresh start.*

I wander into my studio before heading downstairs, collect the empty bottles and tuck them into the recycling in the kitchen. The tile is cool under my bare feet. I stand in front of the fridge for five full minutes but nothing appeals to me. Finally, I make a toast and nibble it while waiting for a cup of tea to steep. The small yellow teapot was a gift from my grandmother when I'd graduated university. How old would Nonna be now?

I remember her as she used to be: bright, dark expressive eyes, long gray hair twisted into a neat chignon. She was always stylish, beautifully put together, even after her body became riddled with cancer. She'd sent me on errands then, when she was too weak. To Nordstrom's or another department store, to buy beautiful but simple housecoats and slippers made of satin. I smile, remembering her feistiness. It lasted way up until the end.

The tea is dark, and I pour a steaming cup, balance it on a white saucer lined with daisies. These cups don't fit this house but I couldn't bear to see them go. So much of what I brought with me to the States from home is gone now. It feels like bits of me have fallen away with each piece of detritus.

A robin outside the window pecks at the still frozen earth. The first sign of spring, isn't it? I shiver, draw up my cold feet underneath me at the breakfast nook and push the rest of the toast away. The teacup warms my fingers which are wrapped tightly around it. An anchor in a cold bay.

Today, I will go to the library that St. Albans and Swanton share: the Franklin County Free Library. Not that I'm expecting any books to announce that my neighbors are practicing the dark arts, but perhaps there is something about the history of this property or the people who lived here before me. I sip my tea for a few more minutes and watch the small brown bird pecking repeatedly. I can relate. Doing something, even something unproductive, feels much better than nothing.

I climb into the Lexus forty minutes later and back down the drive. The sun is out and shining full strength, and it lights the gray of the house's exterior. I stare for a moment, mesmerized by the transformation. It looks . . . I search for the word, then laugh when it comes. Pretty. I look closer and notice some green shoots, tendrils coming up around the edges of the front portico.

Unable to resist the greenness, I park and jog up to take a closer look. Thin, valiant green shoots are twining themselves up and around the very outer edges of the rock that forms the front porch. I look closer when I see a small flash of purple. Crocuses. This makes me laugh out loud. Spring really is here. Sliding back into the driver's seat, I feel excitement bubbling. Hope. Just what I need today.

The library is located on Route 7, the main artery that joins the two towns. It's a busy road lined with older homes, neat yards and signs that announce the speed limit is forty. Driving that speed, however, earns me a hostile glare from an old woman in a huge boat of a car as she swerves around me in a no passing area. Was that really a middle finger waved in my direction? I smile and give a friendly toot. Nothing is going to dampen my good mood today.

The library building is old and brick, dormant ivy crawls up one side. I imagine in the summer that it's a verdant green and that flowers drip from the scroll-edged window boxes. I park in the rear lot, bringing my notebook and pen with me.

The doors open early, and there are already several patrons using the shared computers and browsing tall book stacks when I arrive. Sun slants in through the floor-to-ceiling windows and lights the shelves of books. Dust motes float in the air, and I stop for a moment near the circulation desk to watch them dance.

"Can I help you?" A young woman with a thick silver nose ring begins emptying the book return box as she talks.

I smile, clutching my notebook to chest.

"Yes. I'm doing some research on a certain area of St. Albans, and I wondered if you had books or old newspapers I could look through."

"You wouldn't want either," she says, heaving a particularly large pile of books and magazines onto the circulation desk. Several magazines are slipping out of the stack, and she pulls them out impatiently, slapping them onto the top of the pile.

"What you'd want to do is look through the microfiche. That will give you all the newspaper archives for the past hundred years or so. You're not going to find anything in a book unless the place you are looking for is a historic marker," she blows at her bangs, her cheeks pooching. "Is it? A historic location I mean."

"No, I don't think so. Microfiche would be great if you have the time to show me how it works. I'm afraid I'm a bit ignorant in that area."

She rolls her eyes, smiling simultaneously. "No normal person knows how it works, don't worry. I only know because I work here. Just give me two minutes, okay?"

I nod, and she heaves a second pile of books onto the desk, grumbling as they tip and weave. Finally, content that they aren't going anywhere, she uses her scanning wand and checks each one in, a rapid succession of returns.

She grabs a paper coffee cup. "Come this way," she says and passes through the half door separating the front desk from the rest of the room. Her hair looks partially matted, as though she's working on dread locks. I want to ask, but what if she just doesn't like to brush her hair?

We walk down well-lit stairs to the basement. Tucked into the corner of a room that smells of dry paper and more faintly, of must, is a huge beast of a machine.

"It's right here," the young woman says, plopping down into the plastic molded chair. "Let me just get it fired up."

The machine indeed sounds like it's literally firing. There is a soft creaking and whooshing sound and then some rapid clicks, like a lighter. Finally a low hum fills the air.

"Here we go. Now, what time period are you looking for?"

"Time period?" I blank.

"Is there a particular event you're trying to find?" She restates the question. Am I imagining that her voice is slower, more enunciated?

"Well, actually. Ummm, not really. It's more of a place. The gated community on the hill. Hawthorne Estates. I wanted to learn more about it."

The girl stares at me for a moment. Her face is motionless, and I can't read anything in her expression. Then, slowly, she shakes her head.

"Yeah, I know that place. It was built about twenty years ago. Smith, Paul? John? Some Smith guy was the contractor. He was a pretty popular builder during that time, built a lot of the houses in Franklin County."

She pauses, pushes her hair away from her face and leans back in the chair, thinking. I worry for an instant that she's going to want to know more about why I'm researching this, but she doesn't ask. Instead she sips her coffee, then moves to a cart with narrow drawers and opens one. Tracing a long, white finger along the spines of the boxes inside, she pulls one out and inserts it into the machine.

"This is probably roughly the time period you're looking for. The rolls of film are separated in quarters, so most of this roll will be the spring of that year. I don't know," she pauses from fiddling with the film to look at me. "Spring just seems like the best choice. Lots of building going on, you know?"

I nod. Makes sense to me.

"There you go," she says a minute later. "All set. Now sit here, and I'll show you how to make the film move."

After a quick ten minute lesson on the intricacies of the microfiche machine and how to load and unload rolls of film, the young librarian leaves me to my research.

"I'm right upstairs if you need anything or get stuck," she says. "Or I will be, after a quick smoke break."

"Thanks very much. I'll try not to be a bother."

She shrugs. "You won't be. It's good for me to remember how to use all this equipment. We don't get many people wanting to these days." Her footsteps retreat and I try not to let the silence of the room unnerve me. It's dimly lit here, unlike the brightness of the stairway, and I find myself looking over my shoulder every few minutes.

"Stop it, you're being silly." The words are louder than I intended, and I look around again, just to make sure that no one's watching me talking to myself. The place is deserted.

Refocusing on the task at hand, I move first slowly, then more rapidly through the rolls of film. It takes a few minutes for my eyes to adjust, but once they do I can scan more quickly.

"Gas Wars between Two Main Street Competitors!" a headline screams in bold, black letters. A photo underneath it shows two small town gas stations, with signs boasting, $.99 per gallon. Those were the days.

I continue scanning, seeing advertisements for funeral homes, restaurant specials on locally caught Perch and used car sales. The news stories are typical small town fare: Paul Boucher is honored with medal at local Lion's Club; a blood drive is held at the local elementary school. Patty Minch, a twenty-three year old, was arrested for a second count of DUI and child endangerment. It turns out she had her three-month-old and six-year-old in the car with her when she veered across traffic and plowed into a sign for cigarettes at the local mom and pop gas station.

I don't see anything about anyone named Smith until nearly the end of the roll. My eyes are beginning to cross from the speed of the microfiche when I spot it. Moving too fast, I have to backtrack, slowly, to read the article. It's short, a single paragraph.

"James E. Smith, head of local contracting company Smith Enterprises, has won the bid for construction of Hawthorne Estates, a private gated community to be built off Reynolds Road in St. Albans. Smith states that the project will commence next Wednesday with a dedication ceremony. All are invited to attend the event. Hot dogs, maple cones and cider will be served, and there will be an official ribbon cutting by the mayor."

I move forward to the next week's newspaper, skimming the Thursday edition, but there is no mention of the event. I move forward to Friday and stop immediately when I see the front page.

"Smith's 'Hawthorne Estates' Causes Native Unrest."

{Chapter Thirteen}

My heart pounds in my chest as I read the article that follows, fingers pressing against my lips barely cover the sound of my jagged breathing.

"Members from the Franklin County Abenaki Council attended the Hawthorne Estates dedication ceremony on Wednesday, April 7th in protest. The Abenaki council members, two men and one woman, insisted that the ground was sacred and that digging it would disturb a burial ground of The People."

A grainy photo above the article shows two men with dark hair and light eyes in jeans and button-down shirts. A third figure, the woman I guess, is looking away from the camera and partially obscured by the man in front of her. Another man, the caption states it's Smith, looks as though someone just told him there was a hairball in his soup. His face, even in the black and white photo, looks flushed. I continue reading.

"James E. Smith, owner of Smith Enterprises, recently won the bid for beginning work at the site off Reynolds Road. He stated, 'I have no doubt that this construction will go through as planned. Of course, we will look into this matter in great detail and with thoroughness. However, in my mind this is yet another instance of individuals with a traditional mindset hoping to slow the progress of those dedicated to change.'

"It is not known why the Abenaki council members waited until such a late date to voice their concerns over the tribal burial ground. The issue will arrive on the governor's desk today. Both sides in this situation hope for a swift ruling. The groundbreaking for the new gated community is set for April 15th."

I sit back in the chair, hard plastic fitting comfortably against my back propping me up. My heart has slowed its beating a bit but my brain whirs. Could it be true? A burial ground. Goosebumps skitter up and down my arms and neck. The events from the last few days . . . but what would that mean? Ghosts and spirits. Hauntings. I close my eyes and see the woman from the woods. Her eyes, clear and direct, the shadow playing along the planes of her high cheekbones. The threads of silver hair.

I shake my head, trying to clear it, to stop the onslaught of questions for two minutes so I can think clearly, rationally. It doesn't work. I stand, remove myself from the microfiche machine. It continues to hum loudly.

Drawn to a bay of half-windows, I stare out at the ground at eye-level. They would let in a bit of light normally, but the sun from earlier this morning is gone, covered over with a thick layer of gray clouds. I look for several long minutes, willing the sun to shoot rays in my direction. To warm me.

None appear.

Is the woman I saw in the woods, the ghost, part of this? The words "native unrest" and "burial ground" ricochet around in my mind for several moments as I stare at the sidewalk outside the building. It's empty except for an occasional dry leaf skittering past.

Finally, I return to the machine. The rest of the roll of film runs out before another mention of the contractor or tribal council. Replacing this roll with the next in sequential order, I begin scrolling again. There, on April 13th, another front page article, this one short without a photo.

"Word has come from the governor's office that the construction set to begin on Hawthorne Estates just outside of St. Albans Town will proceed as planned. Governor Johnson states that there is no valid evidence to support the Abenaki claim that a burial ground exists on the premises. State officials did walk the grounds with members of the council, according to a spokesman from the governor's office. Preliminary digging was done at the site. The official report states that the ground at the site was previously disturbed, likely from a recent thunderstorm where a nearby tree was struck by lightning. However, no evidence of human remains was found.

"Phone calls to the council were not returned to press members at the time of this article. Developer James E. Smith was enthusiastic about the start of the project. 'I'm pleased with the results of this investigation, of course,' James said. 'I hope that we can proceed without further delay.' The project is set to commence on April 15th as scheduled."

I read through the files for another hour, but find no other mention of either Hawthorne Estates or the pre-building site. Stretching my arms and legs reminds me that I've been sitting for too long. My body is stiff, and my stomach whines that breakfast was too small and long ago.

I lean forward in my chair, ready to turn off the machine when another article catches my eye. "House fire at Hawthorne Estate destroys family home."

When I nose my car into the driveway of Alicia Gray, the sister of the woman whose family home was destroyed in the fire, the afternoon sun is beginning to fade. Town records led me to the deed of the Rainville family. Rebecca and Kyle Rainville and their two girls lived in the home which burned to the ground. Though the town records showed none of the information about the fire or the family's relatives, the two women working behind the high, wood desk were happy to fill me in. The whereabouts of the Rainvilles now, however, was a mystery.

I finish the last two bites of my apple, that and a sandwich grabbed at the local quick stop were lunch, and wipe my mouth on a paper napkin. The food sits hard in my belly, a far cry from the lunch I could have enjoyed at Grace's. I pop in a breath mint, check my reflection for stray bits of food and, finding none, walk to the house.

This is a suburb of the city. Calling St. Albans a city, after living in London and Philadelphia, still feels like a stretch. Tidy houses march up and down the tree-lined street. The trees are mature, towering above the sidewalk. The houses themselves are older, more dignified than the new developments sprouting up in cow fields across the county. There is ambience here, and landscaping and actual semi-privacy between neighbors.

I like the cozy feel of this neighborhood very much. Something about it reminds me of England. The tidiness, I suppose. Lawns here, despite being brown this time of year, are flanked with hedges and edged gardens which I suspect will showcase gorgeous blooms next month.

Alicia Gray's house, if the scrap of paper in my hand is correct, is a tidy white cape with a gray roof, black shutters and a yellow door. The path to the front door is lined with bare-branched shrubs. I take a deep breath and ring the bell. Chimes sound throughout the house as though small bells are ringing in each room. I wait for several seconds then press the button again.

I'm about to turn back and retrace my steps to the car when the door opens a crack. A gray woman stares out at me.

"What do you want?" Her voice is hollow, hard.

"I'm sorry to bother you. I'm Sarah Solomon. I live in Hawthorne Estates, and I just wanted to ask you something about your family," I pause, clear my suddenly dry throat. "Your sister, Rebecca. Do you have a moment?"

The woman closes the door, hard, in my face.

{Chapter Fourteen}

A second later the door opens again, and I realize she's removed the chain. She waves a limp hand toward the entryway.

"You can come in. Just for a minute though. I'm busy."

"Of course," I murmur, moving through the door. "Thank you so much for your time."

The scent of lemon Pledge and bleach nearly knocks me over. To say the house is immaculate would be a lie. It glistens. Highly polished hardwood floors run throughout the bottom floor, and a white-spindled banister with dangerously shined stairs leads to the upper level of the house. The rooms are small but open, flowing one into the other. Stainless steel and white are the only colors in the kitchen where Alicia leads me. The countertops, also white, are spotless. There are no appliances on the countertop. No dishes in the sink. How do they make toast?

"Really, I'm so grateful to you for taking the time to talk to me. I can only imagine how hard this must be for you."

Alicia snorts.

"They aren't dead, you know."

I pause, momentarily losing my mental balance.

"Excuse me?"

"They aren't dead. Sure it's horrible what happened to them, but you sound like they were murdered in their beds."

"Of course not," I stumble, unsure what to say next.

Alicia smoothes her already perfect gray hair and then points to a high white stool at the bar. I clamber up. She stands across the bar from me, hands held lightly on the counter. Her skin looks dingy against the countertop. She rubs her hands, and I notice the dryness. They make a rough sound as they move against each other.

"My sister, Rebecca, she and I have never seen eye-to-eye. I told her not to move into that place to begin with. It's . . ." her voice trailed off as she stared at a spot above my head. "It's not right."

"What's not right?" My voice sounds overeager, but I can't rein it in. "That's what I'm trying to figure out. I live there, and strange things have been happening. I just came from the library where I was reading old articles and . . ." my voice drifts off as Alicia's gaze turns toward me. Her eyes, so light blue they are nearly white, stare hard into mine.

"You know then." She says it simply, and in that moment a piece of what I've been dancing around, a bit of information that's been standing just beyond my view, drops neatly into place.

"I do?" I want her to tell me. Spell it out.

"You know," she leans forward, elbows on the counter, her face within a foot of mine, "that it's an unholy place. Evil. Dark. Whatever you want to call it. There's something bad up there, and it's not the water."

She looks out the nearby bay of windows quickly, and I realize what animal it is she reminds me of. A bird. A small, gray bird. Her face, illuminated by the windows looks younger to me for a moment, and I imagine when she was young she was beautiful.

"It's devil worship." Her words break the moment of silence quickly, like the seconds after a glass shatters on the kitchen floor. "That's what I believe. What Rebecca thinks. Some people say that it's a coven, witches. And still others," Alicia looks directly at me again, gauging my reaction, "say that the place is haunted by the dead Abenaki that were laid to rest there years ago."

I breathe out slowly through my partially open mouth. My tongue is so dry that the mint I popped earlier feels gritty, stuck to the roof of my mouth.

"Is that what you think?"

She shrugs.

"But there were no remains found. No bodies." I swallow again. "Is that what you believe?" I ask again.

She glances down at her hands. She rubs them together. *Scratch. Scratch-scratch.*

"Yes."

"And is that what your sister Rebecca thought?"

"No. Not at first, anyway."

"But later, she did?"

"Here's what I know," Alicia says. She holds one gray finger up, "There is no way that their house burned down on its own. Why would it? Every other house in the neighborhood was built by the same company, the same builders. Why her house?"

"It could happen," I say, then hurry on when I see her frown and begin to shake her head. "Different wiring used, different raw materials."

"He buys in bulk; all those houses used the same material. Smith. He's a mercenary for sure, but he does quality work. No other house he's ever built burned to the ground. Just my sister's."

"So, you think it was arson?"

"I do." Alicia moves closer to the counter again, pressing her palms into it as though molding it into her flesh. Her fingers flatten and squish against the hardness, turning white around her knuckles. She wears no rings.

"Her neighbors did it. They wanted her out of there with a passion. Every other person in that development was handpicked by him," she spits the last word out as though it's bitter. "All of them except for Rebecca and Kyle."

The stool is hard against my backside. A grandfather clock in the living room ticks loudly.

"By him, you mean Mr. Smith?"

"No," Alicia shakes her head disagreeing. "Him being Dr. Bevins."

{Chapter Fifteen}

When I leave the pristine white house, my head is spinning in circles again. Like tires in the snow, my brain tries to dig into information that sends it skidding and sliding. I get into the car, driving without really seeing, then retrace the route back to my house on autopilot.

The security guard, Byron, lets me through with a wave of his gloved hand. The small, tastefully appointed guard house looks like a miniature version of one of the homes in the community. A child's playhouse.

When I arrive in front of my house, I can't force myself out of the car. I have no idea if Cole is home, or if so, what I will say to him. The cold strangeness of the house, the eeriness of all that's been said about Hawthorne Acres in the last few days, causes shivers even with the heat blowing full force.

I can't do it.

Seconds later I'm on my way to Swanton hoping I might catch John Running Bear at the information center. He's not supposed to be there until tomorrow, but maybe. . . I could use the warmth of the little room. I imagine the potbelly stove pumping heat, the mismatched chairs and the woven rug.

Minutes later, I exhale in relief seeing the old rusted truck parked cockeyed outside the squat building. I pull in beside it, and flee my car, not bothering to lock the door or pull on my gloves.

The chilly air outside reminds me that winter isn't over yet. Rays of anemic sunlight filter through bare branches to the west. The sun will be setting soon.

I move quickly into the information center, a smile on my face, but stop in my tracks when I see two men standing around the high desk where John sat last time I was here.

The men turn slowly. One is big and beefy, his hair dark and short under a dirty John Deere hat. The other is lanky, his clothes comfortable but clean, his eyes hooded under thick brows. Both sets of eyes are ice blue.

The lanky man speaks first.

"You lookin' for John?"

I nod, closing the door behind me. My teeth want to start chattering again, but I clench my jaw and try to force another smile. I probably look deranged.

"He'll be back in a minute. Ole Bailey had to take a . . ." his voice trails off then restarts. "Had to use the outdoor facilities."

"Thanks," I say. I pretend to look at some of the animal skeletons on the wall, hoping that either John will appear immediately or the men will go back to talking about whatever I interrupted. Neither happens.

Finally, desperate to break the awkward silence, I turn back to them. They are still looking at me, not in an ogling, disrespectful way, just studying me like an animal that they can't quite place.

"Are you from the area?" I ask. My voice sounds high and tinny.

"Yup," says the bigger man. "Brothers. Born and raised."

"Ah," I say. "I'm actually doing a bit of research into the Abenaki culture."

The men glance at each other then back at me. The lanky one smiles. It's a kind smile, neither menacing nor patronizing.

"That's good," he says. "It's nice that folks are still interested in learning about The People."

I nod.

"Anything in particular you're studying?"

"No, I just, you know," my voice stumbles. "Just general information. The history of Abenaki in the area of Franklin County."

The back door squeaks, and John's bulk fills the space. In his arms rests Bailey, his sad eyes filmy. John moves into the room, setting the dog on a pillow near the stove, tucking a blanket up and over him. His hands are gentle, like a mother arranging a sleeping baby's bed clothes. For some reason, it brings tears to my eyes. I turn away, look again at the animal skeletons, then move toward the front of the building wiping my eyes roughly as I stare out at the parking lot bordering Route 7.

The men talk quietly for a few minutes then move toward the front door. The one with the John Deere hat removes it momentarily.

"Ma'am," he says.

The other offers a slow wave and a slower smile.

I smile in return, nod my head at each of them.

"Good luck with your research," the first one says. They step through the door, the cold air blowing in momentarily until it's closed firmly behind them.

I turn back to the high counter that John has moved behind. He stands stock still, hands on his hips, looking toward me.

"Sarah Solomon," he says without a smile.

"Yes, it's me. Back to bother you for more information."

"You're no bother," he says. "Sorry, I'm not feeling much like myself today. Old Bailey," he looks toward the dog, then his voice drifts off. I think for a moment he might cry, and I move involuntarily toward him. He doesn't though, and I stop before I reach the desk.

"Don't think it will be long now before I have to call the vet. I've had that dog since he was a pup. He was an excellent hunting dog and a better friend." His eyes look down to the counter, one large finger tracing invisible circles on the scarred desk.

He sighs, and it sounds like the sound that a bear would make: deep, heavy and full. I want to say something comforting, anything really, but no words come.

John wipes a hand over his face, then straightens. "Sorry," he says again. "I don't mean to burden you with my troubles. What can I help you with?"

"You're not. Burdening me, I mean. I think that Bailey is a very lucky dog," I say, looking toward the weary frame on the pillow. "It tells a lot about a person's character, how they treat pets, particularly old ones."

John smiles, and it brings light into his eyes. The sad downturn of his lips for a moment disappears.

"Thank you, Sarah. Now," he slaps his hands against the high desk, and leans slightly toward me, "tell me, what brought you here today? My stellar good looks, charming personality, or amazing conversational abilities?"

I smile, wanting to change the mood in the room as much as John does.

"I have questions," I say. "Many more questions." John's eyebrows raise, but he says nothing.

"The Abenaki were disputing the development of the property, Hawthorne Estates, where I live. They said," the words stick in my throat, "there was a burial ground there. And then there was a fire a couple of years later, after the houses were built; it completely destroyed the home of the Rainvilles. I went to see their kin and . . ." John's eyebrows are raised, and he gives me a 'slow down' motion with his hand.

"Take a breath, Sarah."

I do, just one and then give him a condensed version of the conversation I had with Alicia Gray.

"Everyone in town seems to believe that our neighborhood is, I don't know," I bite my lip, looking past the big man to the far wall. "Evil. Haunted. Demon-possessed. Take your pick."

The room is silent for a moment other than the cracking pops emanating from the fireplace and the slow, deep breath of Bailey.

"What do *you* believe?" John asks.

"I don't know." I stare out the window at the far end of the building facing the street. A group of three school children pass, one on a bicycle, the other two wearing backpacks nearly as big as they are.

"Well, I guess that I do believe something," I say. "Know something. I just can't make out what's truth and what's my imagination playing tricks on me." For one brief moment I think of telling John about what happened in Philadelphia. About the medicine I take every morning to make sure that I stay on an even kilter. And is it? Would I know if I were going crazy again? Would I recognize the symptoms?

"So, tell me what you know. I'll help you sort out the fact and fiction. I'm pretty good at it," John says. "But first, let's get you a chair and something to drink. Brandy okay?" I glance back quickly, just in time to see his eyes laughing at me. "Just kidding. We Indians try not to hit the moonshine at work. Bad PR.

"I can offer you," he stoops to a mini fridge I hadn't noticed before behind the high counter, "a Coke, a diet Snapple or some raw fish." His head peeks over the counter with a grin. "The guys who were just in here did a little late season ice fishing."

I nod. "Snapple, please."

We settle into two chairs near the fireplace, Bailey snores softly on his pillow between us. I tell

John everything. Not about what happened to me, not about the medication or the fact that it now requires more than one glass of Merlot to get through the day but the other things, the things that have been happening at the big gray house. The threats. The fear.

I don't mean to say any of it, but once the words come they won't stop. I'm like a valve stuck in the on position. Part of me, my English part no doubt, is aghast. Another part of me feels nothing but relief. I've been holding in breath I didn't even know existed, and it feels wonderful to let it out.

Twenty minutes later, John pokes the fire. Sparks inside the little stove burst with a loud pop, and I jump. "Sorry," he says and replaces the fire poker near the wall. "Didn't mean to make you more nervous."

"It's okay. I actually feel better now than I have in weeks."

"I want to ask you something, Sarah, and it might sound bad. I mean, it might sound like it's none of my business, probably because it's not."

John frowns, pulling at his chin and staring into the fire. When he looks at me, his eyes reflect the light; it dances and shimmers across his irises. His lashes are black and long.

"Where is your husband in all this?"

I sink back in my chair, the breath leaving my body. This wasn't a question I was expecting.

I'd left Cole out of the story. Why? Because I was still angry at him. Because I felt so unsupported, so defensive. Or was it because of something else? I can't look at John. I stare at my hands which clutch the bottle of iced tea as though I'm strangling it. My fingers are white and spread out over the glass.

"I'm not sure," I say.

There's only silence.

I take a quick peek at John, and he's looking at me, studying me like he did the fire. I don't like it and squirm in my seat.

Long moments of silence pass. I continue to stare at the bottle in my hands. Finally a voice that I barely recognize as my own speaks.

"I've had problems in the past, emotional issues. I was sick and Cole took care of me, gave me everything I needed. He stood by my side, and I'm so grateful for that. I had just launched my own brick and mortar store in Philadelphia for my artwork. It was a big deal to me. Huge, in fact. It was my lifelong dream, and Cole helped make it happen. But then . . ." my voice drifts off. I close my eyes for a moment, willing myself to stay here, in the present, in this room. Not to allow myself even one moment back in that dark place. The place I once feared I'd never find my way out of.

For some unknown reason, a fragment of a prayer my Sunday school teacher taught me in the second grade floats into my head. "May angels watch me through the night, and wake me with the morning light." That time was the night to me, a night that never seemed to end.

{Chapter Sixteen}

I gave John an outline of that time without going into detail. About the weeks I'd been out of commission, the decision to move here to Vermont.

"Cole thought the change of pace and scenery would help me. We'd both get a fresh start. And in a way, it has. It's just that when I explained all these strange things happening at the house, he didn't believe me. He didn't say that, but I could tell. He thinks I'm imagining things. Seeing things that aren't there. Playing the part of a tortured artist, I guess."

I pause, take a sip of tea. My hands tremble slightly raising the bottle to my lips. I hope John doesn't notice.

"I'm sorry," he says after another minute of quiet. "It's really none of my business."

I nod, smile absently into the fire.

"So, let's talk about the facts of this case as we know them." John's voice rises an octave, and he leans back in his chair. Whatever there was between us, the warmth, dissipates. I'm not sure if I'm relieved or saddened.

"We have a case?"

"Sorry. I'm a big CSI fan. Let me have a little fun with it, okay?"

I nod. A small smile emerges. "OK."

We spend the next half hour creating a timeline of events. John finds scrap paper and tapes miscellaneous pieces together, creating one long sheet as I tell him the when and where of each mark to place on the page. Next, he adds in this new information about the fire at Hawthorne Estates and the involvement, however minimal, of the governor and state officials at the time, making notes on the timeline as he goes. He's right. He is good at this, and it is in fact, sort of fun.

"What do you think happened at the building site?" I ask after he's scotch taped the snake-like piece of paper to the wall. "Was it a burial site?"

John rubs his forehead.

"Could be. But truthfully? I'm not sure. The Abenaki as a people have many wonderful traits, but organization isn't one of them. There are so many different opinions and ideas and plans of action that at times it immobilizes us. Our records are minimal, based mostly on the oral history of those who came before us. That's fine within a tribe, but it's difficult when those outside it are involved. Particularly those in government."

"And what do you remember about the fire, if anything?"

"Not much. I was living out West at that time. Did a year of college then quit and bummed around for a while. Skied in Colorado, worked at a ranch in North Dakota. From what I remember there was little about it in the news."

"Doesn't that seem odd to you? Wouldn't that normally be front-page worthy?"

John nods slowly. "I suppose it would."

"And wouldn't you think that particularly in a small town the story would be splashed everywhere? I mean, it's not as though serial killers and hit-and-runs and atrocities that other cities deal with on a daily basis are commonplace here. So why the cover-up?"

"Well, we don't know that it was a cover-up. But it is odd, you're right. Course, Smith is a wealthy man, one with a lot of connections. Could be he did a little footwork to make sure there wasn't a lot of bad publicity."

John sits back in his chair, propping one tree trunk sized leg across the other knee. He's staring at the timeline.

"Have you looked into any of the other home owners in your community? You never hear about houses for sale up there, not until yours, anyway. And there never seems to be anyone leaving the neighborhood."

"That sounds ominous."

John smiles.

"Do you know who lived in your house before you? Did you meet them?"

I shake my head.

"Cole took care of all of that. I never saw the house until the day we moved in."

John looks at me, incredulous.

"It's not the way my life normally works, if that's what you're thinking. I have plenty of opinions and am a full supporter of women's rights and all of that. It's just," I sigh. "I was in a very different place then—mentally, emotionally—so Cole took care of the details."

"Good thing you clarified," John says, cocking one eyebrow. "I almost mistook you for one of those society ladies whose sole job is to attend tea parties and make sure the servants have her lordship's dinner on the table at five sharp every night."

"No, of course not. His lordship likes to eat at six-thirty." We both laugh, and then I stand and gather my purse and the empty iced tea bottle.

"I should go."

Gray light presses against the front windows. Car lights cut through it, moving up and down the main street.

"I think we'd better assign homework," John says, walking with me toward the door.

"You research your neighbors. Try to find out who's moved in or out since the community was built. And try to connect with Alicia Gray's sister. Did the old woman give you a phone number or anything?"

"Email address," I say. "Though it took quite a lot of my English charm to get it."

"Do the English have charm?" John laughs without waiting for a response. "Good, that's good. I'll look into the Tribal Council's involvement in the land, the burial site. I bet there are still some old-timers who can help."

"Wonderful," I say, hand on the doorknob. "Thank you so much, John. I really appreciate your listening and," I wave a hand through the air, "everything."

"Hey, I'm in high demand as a stripper, but I like to take time from my busy schedule to help the little people."

He chuckles, and I can't help but laugh again.

I stop at the house to see if I can repair the damage of last night's fight with Cole, but he isn't there. A note is propped by a vase of gorgeous white Calla lilies on the kitchen counter.

"Sarah, I'm so sorry. Talk soon? Love you, Cole."

I hold the note to my chest for a moment, like it's a baby. Warmth spreads, and even though there is still a residue of anger I push it away. Let the apology wash over me like bath water.

I pull out a ceramic travel mug and eat a few biscuits while standing at the stove waiting for the water to heat. Armed with a fresh notepad and two pens, I head back to the town offices to see what I can dig up on my neighbors. Two nights a week they are open until six o'clock, and I've lucked out.

"What exactly are you looking for?" The woman behind the counter asks me. She has a tangle of mousy brown hair and wears a woolen ski sweater featuring flowers and, strangely, the face of a black and white cow. Her pants are stretchy black and covered with lint and dog hair. The nameplate on the high counter reads, "Selma Gadue." I didn't meet her the other day when I was here.

"Selma is it?" I ask brightly, including a radiant smile. "I love that name; is it a family one?"

"No." She offers no other conversation on her end, so I plunge on.

"I live at Hawthorne Estates," I say. "And I'm doing a little research about the area, trying to get my bearings so to speak." I offer another smile. This time it's returned, briefly.

"Sorry," she says, getting up from her rolling office chair and opening the half-door that leads from the public area into the work area. "It's been a really bad day."

I make a sympathetic noise and follow her into a dimly lit room off of the main office. It's dusty, and my nose immediately starts to twitch. There are no windows. Old lamps in miscellaneous stages of falling apart are scattered on bookshelves and banks of horizontal file cabinets.

"Do you ever get the impression that people just don't care? I mean, they just really don't give a rat's ass about anything?" Selma turns to look at me. Tears stand in her eyes.

"What is it?" I ask, taking a step toward her.

"Last night I found an entire litter of kittens on the side of the road in a plastic tub. Someone just tossed them there like they were trash. They didn't even make air holes or anything."

"Oh no. Were they alive?"

"One wasn't," Selma wipes a hand roughly over her eyes, "but the other four were. I have a call in to the local animal shelter, but I'm sure they're already overflowing. The little fur balls are at the vet's now getting checked over. I'm sure that will cost me a pretty penny."

She sighs deeply, her shoulders slump. "Anyway, let me show you where to find the information you're looking for."

In the back corner of the room, a huge book is spread open on a wooden stand.

"This is the deed book. You'll need to look up the property by either owner name or the street address; that way will be easier for you since you're looking for several properties. It'll save you some time. The book will give you a listing of where to find property information in the land records over here," she points to the horizontal file cabinets. "If you run into any trouble, just come out front and get me. I'm here till closing."

I thank Selma. *Should pat her arm or something?* She looks dejected. But she returns to her desk before I move.

It takes a while to find what I'm looking for in the huge tome, but eventually I do, and a little thrill fills me as I locate the records I need in the wide drawers without help. I'm not sure what I'm looking for, so I remove all the folders I think I'll need and bring them to an ancient copier which adds up the pages and prints me a faded receipt. It moves slowly and creaks as it spits out every third page. A sign over the machine tells me to pay at the front desk. Three cents per sheet. It probably costs twenty just for the electricity on the old dinosaur.

After replacing the files and tidying up the area where I had spread everything out, I go out front to pay, clutching a wide stack of copies to my chest.

"Find what you needed?" Selma asks. She's mindlessly picking at the dog hair on her pants, staring out the window.

"Yes, thank you."

She reads the receipt from the copier and tells me my total. I hand over the money, then push a one-hundred dollar bill over the desk.

"What's that for?"

"For the kittens, to help with their medical bills. I'm sorry I don't have more cash on me . . ."

"I can't take that. I could get into trouble." She looks at me, her brown eyes clear. A smile forms on her lips. "Though I greatly appreciate your offer. It's really kind."

I take the bill, hold it high up in the air and let go. It floats down to the nubby brown carpet.

"Ooops. Looks like I lost it. Well, you know what they say, Selma."

"What's that?" she asks, looking from me to the money and back again.

"Finders keepers." I smile.

{Chapter Seventeen}

The sun is sinking in the west over Lake Champlain, fuchsia strips looking electric next to washes of tangerine and lavender. The temperature has warmed up, and there is a steady drip from the melting ice and snow. I've parked outside the library and maneuver the sidewalk carefully, arms filled with my paperwork haul. A black sign tells me that it's open until nine o'clock.

The space is quiet. A few older people read side by side at one of the oak tables, and two teens whisper at a computer in the corner. It smells nice in here, a mix of fresh pine and a floral scent that I can't place. No one is at the desk when I arrive, but I hear movement in a room marked, "Employees Only." I spread out at one of the heavy wood tables and begin organizing the copies.

There is a lot of information, since the development was built within the past twenty years. Homes original to the area, those that have been standing for one hundred years or more, are much thinner on details. Property lines in these situations often include descriptors like, "from the fencepost on the western side of the pasture to the old oak on the eastern side." But Hawthorne Estates was clearly mapped out, with all dotted "I's" in place and all the "T's" crossed.

As I work my way through the paperwork, I begin taking notes: neighbors' names matched with their addresses, dates the homes were purchased and who completed the sales. I also gather the names of both attorneys involved in the closing.

At the end of an hour and a half, I have a decent size list going. My stomach growls, but I ignore it. Sitting back in the overstuffed chair covered in a hideously patterned fabric with bright orange birds, I study the list.

Nothing sticks out at me. Neighbors moved into the neighborhood around the same time, most just weeks or months after their home was complete. Except . . . I look at the list again. There are no documents further into the future showing that any of the properties changed hands. While living in a home for twenty years isn't an oddity, the fact that no one in this neighborhood has moved certainly is.

Except one—Rebecca and Kyle Rainville— whose house just happened to have burned to the ground less than two years after moving in. I flip through their paperwork. The Rainvilles purchased the house, one near the end of the cul-de-sac, three months after the home was built. Had it stayed empty during that time? A model house, maybe. I push the paperwork around again, flipping quickly. No, here—the previous owner, Wilbur Jennings, was the original owner. I scan the lengthy legal documents and see what I'm looking for: estate.

So Mr. Jennings purchased the house originally, then dies. And then this young family moves in, only to have their house burn to the ground.

Maybe Rebecca can tell me what happened, why they chose not to rebuild in the Estate. There is a house there now, so someone rebuilt. I continue on with the paperwork, looking for the name of the current owner.

My heartbeat increases as the name in bold, black ink stares up at me from the page. Charlotte and Marc Sanders.

After dinner, a nice, quiet dinner in which Cole and I talk civilly to each other, I bundle up. It's dark, but I have a strong torch and the desire to move and get fresh air.

"Did you want to come?" I ask, putting the last dish into the washer and adding soap.

"I was going to, but I'm pretty tired. Mind if I take a rain check?"

"Of course not." I move to him, and he wraps his arms around my waist. He smells of sandalwood.

"What time is your flight out tomorrow?"

"8 a.m., an early one because of the time change. We have to be in Las Vegas for early afternoon. I'm hoping we'll have time to check into the hotel before the meeting, freshen up a little."

I nod, my head moving in slow motion against his chest.

"Sure I can't talk you into coming? The flight isn't fully booked yet, and it would be good for you to. . ."

"To what?" I ask, keeping my voice light. "To stop looking for ghosts in the shadows?"

Cole is silent for a moment. My stomach clenches. Why did I say that?

"I was going to say to get some sun. It's not a long trip, but we could tack a few more days onto it after my meetings. Come with me, Sarah."

He tilts my head back to look into my face. He's so handsome; even after all this time together I sometimes catch my breath. His eyes, a strange grayish green, are looking into mine. His breath moves the hair on my forehead.

It would be good for us to have some time together. To relax and forget about this house and this neighborhood and the people that live here. For a moment I'm tempted to say yes, to watch Cole's eyes light up. To run upstairs and haul out my suitcase.

"I can't," I say. "Not this time. But your next trip I will, I promise."

Cole sighs, kisses my forehead and releases me.

"I'm going to hold you to that."

I nod, smile, and move to the hallway closet to get my coat and boots.

The moon is so full tonight that I don't need the torch. There are little fringes of snow left along the walking path, but most of the earth is bare, littered with leaves and twigs. I smell pine, and the fresh air is incredible. I draw deep breaths in and feel the tight pull in my belly loosen.

It will be April in just a couple of weeks, and though the air around me hovers in the low 40s, I sense that warmer weather is coming. The air smells like greenness, as though the tiny leaves on the trees are pressing their scent into the chilly air, daring it to nip them.

Crocuses, which I hadn't noticed before here, poke up through a tangle of decaying leaves near an old oak tree. I'm tempted to reach out, remove the leaves, but remember a gardening workshop I'd taken years ago.

"They need the protection of the leaves," the old gardener had told the class, pressing around the tiny bunch of purple flowers as though one of Picasso's paintings in the Louvre. "If they're removed, the plants have more of a chance of dying due to exposure from frost, ice, frigid wind. The young plants use the leaves as a sort of sweater."

Tomorrow I'll come back out here, see the crocuses in daylight. Maybe I'll bring a camera or my sketchbook. A little thrill runs through my chest, and for the first time in a long time I feel hopeful. It's been so many months since the thought of making art, creating anything, has brought me a feeling other than dread. A smile wavers on my lips and then secures itself there. It feels good.

Snap.

A branch ahead and to my left breaks neatly in the quiet of the woods. I falter, my steps for a moment uneven until I come to a complete stop. Listening. I quiet my breath, trying to keep it as low and slow as possible.

Rustling to the left again, this time as though something large is moving through many branches. A wolf? Are there any left in this part of the country? Maybe a skunk or fox. Bear? I shiver, look down at my torch and try to remember which bears live in Vermont. Black bears, I think. Are they the ones that run away when you wave your arms and yell, or does that cause them to attack?

I am completely vulnerable standing directly in the moonlit path, so I creep to the right, steps silent as possible. Moving through crunchy leaves, this is a feat. I duck low, moving brambles and branches out of my way as I slip into a small grove of trees and wait.

Watching.

Crack.

Another branch breaks. This one large and closer to the path I just left. My fingers and palms press into the craggy tree bark and for one crazy instant I want to wrap my arms around the tree, hug it as though it's a parent that can protect me from whatever is coming.

My breath quickens. I remember playing moonlight tag on long summer nights on my grandparents' farm. Only there are no giggling cousins hiding nearby.

I hear something low and gravelly.

A voice.

A human.

My body sags in relief against the tree, only to straighten again. Who is out here at night? There are more than one, two at least. Maybe three voices, all low, murmuring. Now many branches are breaking, the sound of twigs scratching against outdoor clothes.

The first person steps out onto the path wearing a dark windbreaker, gray hair tousled.

I nearly scream.

It's Dr. Andrew Bevins.

{Chapter Eighteen}

Bevins pauses, waiting for his companions. He runs a hand over his forehead with a handkerchief. Seconds later another man emerges, but I don't recognize him. He has a dark knit cap pulled low and a thick wool peacoat. They are carrying something between them, something heavy enough that the second man grunts when he mounts the small lip of the walking path.

It's a bag. An extra-long, black duffle. It reminds me of Cole's fencing days; the one he used for his equipment looked similar but slightly smaller.

They stand motionless on the path, looking ahead in the direction I was headed moments ago. Each man holds an end of the bag in gloved hands. Finally, a third person emerges from the woods, this figure slight, voice higher. Blonde curls spill from her stocking cap.

Charlotte.

"It's freezing out here!" She climbs easily out of the brush and onto the path. "I knew I should have worn that thicker coat."

The second man looks over his shoulder at her. His breath comes in small white puffs. He doesn't say anything, doesn't have to. His look is enough to silence her.

". . . need for tomorrow night. It's not far now. . . . keep up with an old man, Marc?" Bevins is speaking but his words are muddled from where I'm standing. My heart is thundering so loudly in my chest; I'm surprised they can't hear it.

I don't hear the second man's response, but assume it's affirmative as they hoist the bag up again and move forward on the path.

"What is this? A twig in my hair?" Charlotte moves behind the men, oblivious to the second man's dark look, working her fingers through her hair. The trio moves forward, slowly creeping through the moonlight.

Seconds later, I sink to my knees, crouching behind the tree, resting my forehead against the bark. My breathing slows after a minute and my heartbeat, while not normal, isn't so erratic.

What are they doing out here? And what is in that bag? The thought sends goose bumps racing up my arms and back. Should I follow them? If I'm quiet. . .

I look around the woods. It will be hard to stay hidden with the moonlight so bright. And I'm not exactly dressed for stealth. My jacket is navy blue, but I've left on my chinos and my ivory-colored hat and scarf practically glow in the night air. I don't realize I'm chewing the inside of my lip until I taste blood.

I can't. Whatever they're doing, it's none of my business. I square my shoulders, relief flooding through me like a physical wave of warmth. But at the back of my mind is a small voice. *What if there's a person in there? What if it were you? Or Cole.*

My mind is telling that voice to shut up, to go instead back to my warm bed and forget about whatever it is my neighbors are doing or planning to do. Already I can feel the heat of bathwater covering my cold skin, see the hot tea steaming from the pot.

I sigh, push myself up. Arguing with this voice is futile. Using the tree as a stabilizer, I move out toward the path but don't walk on it, staying instead to the right partially hidden by the low brush. Walking this way makes me twice as slow. I have to pause to go around low branches, brambles and clumps of dead leaves. Still, I'm not as visible. If the trio comes back this way, I can duck back into the trees and remain hidden. I hope so, anyway.

Moving silently through the leaves is impossible. They crunch noisily underfoot. Should I take off my boots? Snow still laces the sides of the wood like ribbons of icing. I leave them on and move a little closer to the path where there are less dead leaves.

The three figures in front of me are barely visible and I pray that they don't look back for any reason. There's a quick tinkle of laughter from Charlotte and then a low, loud expletive from one of the men. My bet is on Marc—her husband. *Thank you, Charlotte.* Her chattering is probably covering up the noise of my feet.

We walk on, another ten minutes at least. Should I go back, rouse Cole? But then the trio stops and makes a sharp left into the woods. I hang back, nervously picking at the hem of my coat sleeve, my right hand on my torch. What would I even do with it? In a time of duress it could make somewhat of a decent weapon, I suppose. Provided my attacker doesn't have something more sophisticated like a knife or gun.

Best not to think about that.

I creep forward, using the trees as cover. The three went off the path and are nowhere in sight. Naked branches scratch at my face and coat. I hold my hands up, pushing them out of my way.

The light of the moon disappears temporarily as heavy clouds press against it. Where have they gone? I stumble, my foot catching the upward u-shape of a root. Instinctively, my hands go out. The torch tumbles. Without thinking, I crouch and catch it seconds before it crashes into the dry leaves underfoot. I stay in that position a minute, hands shaky, relief washing itself over me.

Squatting in the same crouch a moment later, I realize that I can't hear the group anymore. Their footsteps have faded away completely, and there is no sound of them moving through the woods. Either they've stopped nearby or have moved so far into the forest that I can't hear them.

Standing, my knees are stiff from the cold and awkward gait required by the undergrowth. The moon has slipped behind a curtain of clouds. I don't dare turn on my torch, but it's incredibly difficult to see where I'm going. The gravel path is just visible, a dark gray ribbon against the blackness of the forest floor. I follow alongside it like a river, turning where I think the group might have.

A yank on my hair brings tears to my eyes, and my hat falls to the ground. I lose a minute untangling the strands from a low-hanging branch. I can barely see the path to my right and continue walking deeper into the woods. An owl hoots nearby.

Whooooo? Whooooo?

The sound ricochets around the woods, bouncing off trees until finally falling to the carpeted forest floor.

I stop.

Listen.

No sound.

Where have they gone? I look back over my shoulder to the right. *Where is the walking path?* For a moment I'm frozen, fear taking over.

Whooooo? Whooooo? The owl sounds again as memories unleash in a deluge. It's been so long now, but they are as clear as cut glass in my mind and just as jagged. That night. The cold, the blackness of it pressing against me, the terror and panic. Blue lights dancing in the rear and side view mirrors, dizzyingly hypnotic. More images. These from afterward, from the hospital. The blanket of drug-induced sleep that pulled at me over and over again. Coming up for gasps of consciousness and then sliding back under. Cole sitting at my bedside, crying. But always when these memories come, there is one word that describes them best: blackness.

It's surrounding me, and I cannot see. Thick clouds have rolled over the moon. The air, frosty before, even colder now. My chest tightens, squeezing. I can't breathe. My heart twists and pounds frantically in my chest like a bird beating against the sides of a cage. I recognize the symptoms, know what will happen next.

No, no, no. Not now. Not here.

And then I feel as though I'm floating somewhere above my body, looking down in concern to the Sarah on the floor of the forest. The floating me watches the woman on the ground struggling, straining. And I know what's coming next: the paralysis, the inability to breathe. My heart rate will continue too fast, tapping hard and quick in my chest like machine gun fire. Then the dizziness will increase. I won't be able to draw in a single breath. My chest will tighten and constrict. No air. Then darkness of a different kind will come. Darkness that swallows me up and takes my consciousness. And I will collapse on the moss-covered earth.

And finally, blessedly, all will be quiet.

{Chapter Nineteen}

When I come to, the moon has reappeared. A stick pokes painfully into my left leg, and I see that I've fallen between two pine trees. Moss sticks to my face, and stray leaves tangle in my hair. I stay on my side for a moment, assessing. I'm not hurt but shaking. My breathing has returned to somewhat of a normal state and my heart rate is slowing.

The panic attacks started after that night in Philadelphia. I haven't had one this bad in months, though. The medicine helps. Psychotherapy was supposed to help, but I gave up after a couple sessions.

I prop myself up on my hands and knees, then slowly, slowly stand supporting myself against the tree closest to me. Pine pitch makes my palms sticky and releases the smell of Christmas.

I look around again, trying to see the thin ribbon of gray, the walking path. I see only trees and shrubs and the occasional open spot where nests of leaves have blown together. Part of me wants to just sink into a pile, wait until morning to worry about getting out of here. The men and the bag and Charlotte are long gone. There are only normal sounds of a forest at night: an occasional hoot of the owl, the now subdued frogs in the swamp nearby. A breeze moves tree branches together, sighing between them like a human thing.

Wait.
The owl.
Whoooo?

I can't be far off course. I close my eyes, listen hard. Wait two minutes, five. There, the owl sounds again, to the left. I move slowly in that direction, keeping my footsteps as quiet as possible, listening. It could be a different owl. It could be the same owl, but it's maybe flown in an entirely different direction. It could, though, be a way out. I walk about thirty paces, then hear him again a bit louder. I continue in that direction.

Another five minutes, and I emerge from the trees back onto the path. I scramble up the incline, sighing with relief as my feet hit the gravel. The moon is shining, big and round, and I walk fast back toward the house.

I can't stop thinking about the bag. I see it as I get ready for bed, pulling bits of dry leaves and a small twig from my hair in front of the mirror. My cheeks are still pink from the chilly air, cold to the touch. Still, I smile, grateful to be safe and sound in a house that just a day earlier didn't feel either safe or sound.

As I slip under the covers, an owl hoots, low and far off. Cole, still sleeping, wraps an arm around my waist. I burrow next to him, his warmth seeping into my cold limbs. But when I close my eyes I see the face of Andrew Bevins and a black, oversized duffle bag.

The next morning I sleep until almost ten o'clock. Sunlight pokes me incessantly in the face, squeezing beneath closed eyelids until I finally give up. Feet hit cold floor, toes grope for slippers.

Coffee. Now.

Padding to the kitchen, I see through bleary eyes a note from Cole propped on the coffee maker. He's out of state for the next couple of days; guilt twists my gut sharply. A good wife would have gotten up to see her husband off. I try his cell, but the call goes immediately to voicemail. I leave a message thanking him for the note and wishing him safe travels.

"Cole, I just wanted to tell you also," my voice drifts off for a moment. I think about what I saw in the woods last night. I clear my throat. "Just wanted to tell you that I love you. Please call when you have a chance." Call ended, my phone says as I push the red button to disconnect.

I sit in the breakfast nook sipping strong coffee. Yesterday's idea of returning to the woods to sketch some flowers and photograph some of the trees meanders into my brain. I sip slowly, wondering what else I might find in the woods. Maybe a big, black bag or footprints or something more sinister. I put my empty cup in the sink, take a sip of water and wash down three pills from three different orange bottles. My name is printed neatly on each label. The name of each medicine is printed in all caps, but there is no mention what they are for. I'm glad of that.

Back upstairs and into the walk-in closet, I pull on clean undergarments, jeans and a thick sweater over my t-shirt. I find a pair of wool socks and my hiking boots at the back of the closet. A handheld GPS, a bottle of water and cell phone are tucked into a backpack in under five minutes. There's nothing left to do but go.

The door off the patio closes behind me with a loud thud. The house, it seems, is kicking me out, back into the woods where I very much don't want to go. I straighten my shoulders, dig deep for some of my English grit.

The day is cloudy but bright. I squint and consider going back for sunglasses but don't. Traveling in the daylight is much easier than night, and I move quickly, eyes focused on the path. It takes about fifteen minutes to find the spot where I veered off the path last night. Can that really be true? It feels like I wandered out here for hours. The grass is slightly trampled though, leaves displaced in rows where my sneakers separated them.

I continue down the path, looking carefully at the grass and underbrush on my left, searching for the spot where Charlotte and the men would have walked. The birds' early morning fervor has died down to quiet chirps by the time I find the spot. I'm tilting the water bottle to my lips when I see a broken branch, then another and finally, further out into the woods, the grass trampled. I cap the bottle, return it to my bag. The sun is warm on my neck, and I take off my hat, stuff it into the backpack as well. The air smells of earth, heavy and loamy.

The trampled grass is easy to follow at first, but as the woods become dense, it's more difficult to stay on course. Slowing down, I look for more broken branches. I wish that John Little Bear were here. Given all the hunting he does, I'm sure tracking the ghostly footprints wouldn't be a problem.

A pine branch slips past my hand and slashes me across the cheek and I yelp. The scratch burns, feels hot under my palm. Standing there, a hand pressed to my face, I hear the caw of a crow in a nearby tree. The sun erupts from behind a bank of clouds, and I turn my face up instinctively to its warmth. I breathe deep, enjoying the scent of green growing things and the dark earth under my feet.

When I open my eyes moments later, I take another deep, full breath then exhale, turning in a complete circle. All around me are woods. Everywhere except . . . there. I see something ahead. About a hundred feet out.

A clearing.

It's well protected on all sides from trees and undergrowth. The path to it is narrow and wouldn't be visible from the walking path itself. The grass here is trampled, too, a few footprints still clearly visible in thick mud near the center. I follow the smashed grass, the muddy prints until I come to the entrance of the clearing. Holding my breath, I push through a weeping willow branch that partially obscures my view.

A shiver runs up and down my neck and spine like a column of ants. I notice two things right away. The space is large and completely devoid of trees and saplings. That in itself is strange. The forest, always trying to maintain its own level of growth, always trying to reclaim the land taken from it by human hands—why would this place be exempt from Mother Nature?

But it is the thing I see in the center of the clearing that causes the goose bumps to pop up on the rest of my body. At first it seems unreal, as though I've stumbled onto the set of a movie or outdoor theater production. In the center of the space is something long and flat. A stone. It's light gray, probably granite. It's at least five feet in length, about three feet wide. It stands at waist-height.

I scan the woods around me, pausing for a long moment to look and listen before moving out of the trees into the clearing. Forty paces brings me to the massive stone. I rest my hands against it. It's sun-warmed and smooth, but not polished like a gravestone. There are dark sections along the top. It almost looks as though a different type of stone, something nearer to black in color, has been pressed into the lighter rock.

Crouching, I see that two large stone legs, rudimentary pillars of a sort, support the weight of the flat rock. A bench. But why here? Surely my neighbors aren't secret birdwatchers. A table maybe. For nature picnics. I snort out a half-laugh picturing Andrew Bevins and Charlotte and the others I've infrequently seen in our neighborhood frolicking around the table, daisies woven in their hair.

Definitely not picnics.

What then? I walk around the back of the table which looks very much like the front. I spread my circle out wider, walking around the clearing looking for anything that might tell me why these stones are here. There is no sign of the black bag, no sign that humans were here recently except for the trampled grass.

Why come here? Why haul whatever was in that bag such a great distance, and then what? Bring it back with them?

Standing in the meadow, I realize that something is very wrong in this place. Where the woods were filled with the happy chatter of birds, the sound of a light breeze moving tree branches, here there is no sound at all. No bird calls, no movement of air.

It feels heavy, dead. Goose bumps race up and down my legs and arms again, and despite the warmth of the sun I shiver. I look around the clearing again, stomach clenching. My feet tell me to run.

I turn, ready to bolt, when I see her.

The ghost.

{Chapter Twenty}

Her face is lined and expressionless and her body does not move. Mine, on the other hand, is trembling. I am frozen mid-step, my right foot in the direction of the walking path.

The Abenaki woman stands, barely an outline against the trees in the far side of the clearing furthest from the point where I entered. She's dressed in the same soft leather dress, straight-standing, shoulders thrown back. Her eyes watch me intently, as though a deer spotting a predator. Her hair is black and gray, and strands of it have fallen from the neat braid that is slung over one shoulder like the strap of a handbag.

"Hello?" My voice is small.

No movement. No change in expression.

I take a step, slowly holding my hands out in a universal sign of peace. She is as still as a statue. Another step slowly, then one more. Still no movement. The stone table is behind me now. Excruciatingly ponderous steps, hands remain in front of me, palms up and open.

"It's OK," I tell her. "I'm not going to bother you." I'm close enough now to see the wrinkles in her face. She's older than I initially thought; small folds outline eyes and define crevasses in her cheeks. Her eyes are clear and sharp, though.

"My name is Sarah. Sarah Solomon. I'm just here," I take a quick look back over my shoulder, wave a hand toward the clearing, "to. . ." my voice fades as I look back to the place where the woman stood.

She's gone.

I run to the place where she was standing, then beyond it, crashing through the forest.

"Please," I beg. "Please don't go!"

I've moved deeper into the woods, small branches whip me in the face and shoulders as I run blindly. Panting, I stop several minutes later in a thicket of young trees. Their trunks are slender and graceful. I place a hand against one for balance. It is cool and firm under my palm.

There is no sign of the ghostly woman. Birds call overhead, reminding me that I'm a distance from the clearing. I catch my breath, follow my steps back, moving branches out of my way with my hands spread wide and straight in front of me. It reminds me of party games as a little girl, blindfolded, feeling my way to the piñata or the donkey missing a tail.

There is no sign of the woman near the stone table or anywhere in the clearing. Again I notice that all noise from the woods is silent in this place. I shiver then gather my backpack and move to the tree line where I entered the clearing. I can't bear to stay there but want her to come back. I will her to as I sit cross-legged. Waiting.

She doesn't reappear.

I drink the rest of my water, lean my head against the strong, sure trunk of the willow tree. The fronds reach down to the earth, moving with a barely felt breeze. An airplane buzzes overhead, and I give in, close my eyes. I wait for an hour, then give up, shoulder my pack and retrace my steps home. There are still the papers to go through, deeds and legal paperwork that I gathered from the town office. In all of my recent woodsy adventures, I've forgotten about them.

I shower and change clothes, make a proper breakfast of an egg and toast even though the kitchen clock scolds that it's nearly two o'clock. Sitting in the breakfast nook, I eat the food and then sip a cup of tea, papers and files covering the table. Sun streams in the two banks of windows where the alcove is situated. It's one of the few places in this huge house where I feel comfortable. Birds feast at the group of feeders outside the window. A small garden was created here for them, filled with thick bushes and in the summer, Cole said, flowers that attract hummingbirds and butterflies.

I take another sip of tea. What were the people like who lived here before us? Cole told me it was an elderly man whose wife had died nearly a decade before he sold. Were they happy here? It's hard to believe that they lived in such a modern home, full of stainless steel and long staircases. Did she die here? I shiver.

Pushing the breakfast dishes away, I fumble through the paperwork sorting by house number, low to high. I don't know any of my neighbors' names except for Charlotte, of course, and Dr. Bevins. Nine homes make up Hawthorne Estates, all built within a span of two years. The documents are long and tedious to read, filled with legalese and the words 'wherefore' and 'whereas' sprouting up repeatedly in in the middle of dry paragraphs. I take notes, in part to keep myself awake, on a lined yellow pad. I jot down dates that I think will be important, names of attorneys and notaries, any information on the homeowners themselves which is scarce. I also start to write down the names of the realtors, but by the time I get to the fourth transaction notice something odd. "C. J. St. Francis" and "Cy Francis" show up on each. Brothers? Related at least, maybe cousins. I jot the names down. I can ask my new friend at the Town Office. Or maybe Grace. She seems to know most of the locals.

I flip through the rest of the pages, one by one. The houses were built in reverse order of the house numbers. Meaning ours, number one, was the last built and number nine, owned by Bevins, was the first. What was it Charlotte had said? That he was a psychiatrist, a good one. I make a note on my pad to Google him. There has to be information online about both the man and his medical practice. I jot the other neighbors' names down, too.

Waiting for the kettle to boil again, I stand at the granite counter looking out to the landscaped back yard. Flower stems are starting to poke up through the decayed leaves along a line of mature holly bushes near the inground pool. The pool is covered, twigs and leaves and melting ice floating on the thick protective layer of the tarp-like material. I notice a movement near the line of holly. My eyes dart back.

What in the world. . .

I'm cramming my feet back into hiking boots not bothering to tie the laces and running out the door without my jacket. Something flutters from the holly bush closest to the pool, hidden from view unless one is standing at just the right place in the kitchen. It bends and flutters in the breeze. The sun illuminates the whiteness of it, making it glow. As I approach, I slow my steps taking quick glances to my left and right. This wasn't put here haphazard. It was placed, intentionally.

The breeze moves the white paper again; dancing, it shimmies and moves. A long string, garden string, tethers the paper to the branch. It's a regular piece of copy paper folded in thirds like a letter. I loosen the string, pull it from the neat round paper-punched hole. My hands are shaking. There is no writing on the outside.

I smooth the paper out flat, my fingers running along opposite the creases. A black-and-white photo.

I moan, sink to my knees. My breath comes fast, hitching and tight in lungs that don't want to open.

Then I scream.

{Chapter Twenty-one}

The wet earth presses into my pants and legs chilling them instantly. I barely notice. I clutch the piece of paper in my hands willing myself to look away, to get up, to do something. Instead, I kneel on the wet, cold earth fingers trembling, whimpering.

On the paper are three images. Grainy but clear enough to make out.

The first is a partial copy of a medical chart. The words are small and tight and hard to read except the section that's been circled in red pen. "Admittance to Psych Ward Level III: Sarah Solomon." There's a date, but I don't need to see it to remember. It's burned into my memory like a brand.

The second image is one of me wearing dark sunglasses and a floppy hat stepping from a long, dark Town Car. My hands are up in front of me as though I'm warding off unseen attackers. It was the photographers, reporters with their humiliating questions and microphones jammed into my face that I was trying to fend off. I remember the bright pops of a thousand flashbulbs, the scent of heavy perfume and cologne, of warm bodies pressing close.

The third image is one that I don't recognize, at least not immediately. It is rectangular in shape, the writing in small square letters. Squinting, I read my name. My social security number. My date of birth. And then recognition. It's the hospital band that followed me those dark days. Not the one on my wrist. I burned that when I got out leaving a pile of stinky ash in the pure white toilet. This must be a photocopy of the second one, the version that travels with a patient's medical records around a hospital.

How? How did they get this? And who? My trembling is slowing, and I sink back to my heels, paper still clutched within my tight grasp. I look furtively around; the trees and bushes, are they hiding sneering faces?

"... He's the lead psychiatrist at Jacobs-Smith. . .a man with a lot of power." Charlotte's words last week when she was sitting in my living room. Able to get past medical records on a patient in another city I wonder? Suddenly sick, I put my head between my knees, take steadying breaths. Moments later, my stomach has stopped roiling, and I refold the paper and carry it with stiff fingers into the house as though it's a dead mouse.

Paper stashed deep in the back of a desk drawer in my studio, I strip my clothes and shower again feeling the hot water burn away at least some of the feelings of fear and shame. My mind teases me with images from that dark night, toys with questions about the paper. And the hands that placed it in my garden.

A trick my psychiatrist taught me wanders into my brain, and I grasp at it like a drowning woman. "Picture a light switch, Sarah," her voice is soothing, long blond hair piled up on top of her head. "Imagine the flat, smooth surface. Now slowly, without force, picture your fingers moving toward it." She asks me to close my eyes, and I do. I imagine my shaky white fingers moving toward the white plastic. "Imagine that this switch controls those thoughts and that moving it to the off position will turn them off. You don't have to give in to them, Sarah. You don't have to be controlled by the bad memories. Take your fingers, and turn it off, Sarah." Her voice is soothing, like sinking into a hot bath.

I take a long, deep breath, picturing the switch, hearing it click into the off position in my mind. There are other things to take care of. Things that require lucidity and emotional control.

After I've dressed, I call Grace at the cafe. She's not able to come to the phone, a young woman tells me, sounding out of breath.

"We're super busy right now," she says. "Do you want me to take a message?"

I tell her no, that I'll stop in later. Stuffing the housing paperwork I've been working on into the bag holding my laptop, I grab my keys. The café will be a pleasant distraction and working there in the warm, chaotic and bright space will be good for me. Plus there's a chance Grace will know something about the two realtors.

I've settled into a small table by the window balancing my armload of paperwork with a pottery mug of flavored coffee. On top of the mug is a small lilac-colored plate holding an Apple Bomb, one of Grace's own recipes. The smell of cinnamon and nutmeg and the sharp, dry scent of the coffee make my stomach growl.

The café is busy, most tables are full, and the noise level is high. Conversations at different volumes mix with funky Reggae music. A guy in his mid-twenties sporting multiple tattoos and huge green earrings in each ear, bobs his head along with the music. In front of him are a stack of textbooks. I look more closely. Law books. He moves into playing imaginary drums while I organize things on the table and take my first bite of the decadent pastry. Oh. My.

It's more than a half hour later before Grace finally slides into the seat next to me. The cafe traffic has finally slowed to a dribble, and most of the tables stand empty now.

"Not brothers," she says. Strands of her hair are bright blue, and she wears black-framed cat glasses with rhinestones on the stems. Her flannel shirt is dotted with flour under a grease-stained apron.

"Not brothers," I repeat. "But related?"

She nods. "In a sense," pausing she takes a sip of coffee. "It's the same person: C.J. St. Francis is Cy Francis. He goes by Cy. He's a realtor with Fine Homes. You know the ones with the big yellow signs? There's a branch over on Fourth Avenue, big place."

I nod though I don't know the place.

"So, he's a successful realtor. Do you know anything else about him?"

Grace leans back in her chair. She has a smudge of flour on the side of her chin. "He's Abenaki. There's a long history of Abenaki with that name in the area. In fact," she pauses to rearrange the napkin dispenser, "Homer St. Francis was chief for many years in the early 90s, Swanton area. No relation, though. At least, I don't think so."

I scribble a note on my pad. John might know more.

"So does Cy live around here? Does he work out of the local office?"

I take a sip of coffee while Grace bites into her croissant. Flaky bits fall to the saucer and table like confetti. Inside, a hidden pocket of strawberry compote oozes.

"Nah. Not anymore. He doesn't like to associate with his kin as far as I've heard. Lives up in Shelburne, feels more at home among mansions and golf courses that didn't come from his ancestral background, I guess."

A thought nibbles at the edge of my consciousness.

"There was talk about a burial ground at Hawthorne Estates, wasn't there? I read something about it in my research."

Grace nods. Her lined face looks away from me for a moment, sad eyes looking even sadder.

"I remember that. There was a protest by some of the tribe. Not that it did much good. One of the things I love and hate about living here is the way that things never seem to change."

There's silence between us for a few minutes. Cars slowly pass the bakery windows, making slushy sounds in the dirty snow.

"Do you believe that there were people buried there?"

Grace frowns.

"No graves were ever found. James Smith, the contractor, he had a crew from the State of Vermont go up and do some digging. Said there was no evidence of any sort of ancestral burial grounds up there. But who knows."

"What do the locals think?"

Grace blew breath out, her cheeks pooching for a second.

"Hard to say. Some folks believe it, the older generation. And some of the other old ones wouldn't admit it even if it were true. The Abenaki were treated the same as the French Canadians when they settled here, despised pretty much. Treated like Black people were in the South and like the English in Quebec. Same story different place, I guess." Grace pauses for a sip of her drink, a bite of flaky croissant lands on her apron. She brushes at it absently.

"The younger ones for the most part are intent on either getting out of the state as fast as they can or returning to it to raise their families and build new houses. They don't have time or interest likely, in what happened here a century ago."

"It's like this everywhere it seems. Are we as a race so intent on moving forward that we slam the door on the past and all the lessons it has to teach?" I hesitate and then tell Grace about the nighttime adventure, leaving out the part about the letter flapping in the holly bush.

"You've got to be careful, Sarah. Following people around in the middle of the night? Call me next time. Promise." Her face is concerned, eyes serious behind the glasses and fixed on mine. I nod, look at the table. My mug leaves a ring as I lift it for a sip. A warmth spreads through my chest. It's been a long time since I had someone to confide in. Or I should say, someone who believes me when I confide in them. Our conversation is paused momentarily, as Grace goes to answer a beeping in the kitchen. When she returns I ask, "So this St. Francis guy. He'd be in the yellow pages?"

"Let's see." Grace moves behind the counter and comes back seconds later with a dog-eared copy of a thick phone book.

"Would you like his office or home number?"

I look up, smile.

"I'm not going to call him."

"Then why. . ."

"I'm going to see him in person. With these," I say, shaking the thick stack of papers in my hand. "I'd like to know why he's the only realtor listed. Why he was so intent on selling his ancestral lands, if they were that, to Smith. And I'd like to know how well he knows my neighbors."

Grace shakes her head, but she's smiling, too.

"I like your spunk, Sarah. Just be careful. I don't know Cy well but have heard that he's manipulative, threatening even, if he doesn't get his way."

I nod, put on a brave face.

Inside I'm trembling.

{Chapter Twenty-two}

"Miss Solomon?"

I draw my breath in unconsciously. The most handsome man I've ever seen stands before me, tall with thick, dark hair falling over perfect cheekbones. Clear dark eyes observe me, and a smile forms on lips full enough to make a woman jealous.

I clear my throat.

"It's Misses," I say, tone clipped, overcompensating. I'm suddenly conscious of the curls springing around my head messily.

Cy St. Francis gives a mock bow and extends his arm toward his office. I rise from the plush chair in the waiting area, give a smile to the woman behind the shiny desk who is so busy typing away she ignores me, and then walk ahead of the realtor into his office.

"How can I help you?" Cy asks, settling next to me in a matching club chair. Two are drawn up to an unlit fireplace which houses a stack of birch logs. The office is large with plush Persian carpets on hardwood floors, enormous windows overlooking Lake Champlain and several pieces of antique furniture. I recognize a Davenport desk from the mid-eighteenth century and a Chippendale table, glossy and gleaming in the corner of the room. Business must be good.

"Thank you for taking the time to see me. This may sound odd," I say, pausing to clear my throat, "but I live at Hawthorne Estates in St. Albans."

"Not odd yet," Cy says with a slow smile, "but I assume you're getting to that."

I smile but can tell my face is turning pink. I wish suddenly that I'd worn a proper outfit instead of wrinkled khakis and a button down that I notice, with horror, is sporting a jam stain from breakfast.

You're not in secondary school for pity's sake, Sarah.

"I'm here for some information," I tell Cy and remind myself of my purpose. Straightening my shoulders, I remove the paperwork from my bag, hold it on my crossed leg. "I understand that you were the realtor for all the houses sold in my community."

Cy pauses for a second, nods. Another smile. "That's right, I was."

"And I've been doing some research on the area. There was an article in the paper which referred to the possibility that the land developed was Abenaki."

"And you thought because my last name is St. Francis, I must be Abenaki."

I swallow, my throat suddenly dry.

"No, of course not. But . . . aren't you?"

"Mrs. Solomon, what is it you're getting at? Certainly you didn't travel all the way here to inquire as to my ancestral heritage. I have a lot of appointments today," Cy says. Another easy smile reminds me that he's not at all ruffled by my questions, just a successful man with a busy day ahead of him.

"Of course that's not why I came. I just wondered if you could take a look at these," I set the stack of paperwork in the middle of a small table between us, "and tell me why you're the only realtor involved in the sale of nine houses. And why you would, if you are in fact Abenaki, be willing to help develop land that belonged to your ancestors."

"Ah there we are, back to that question about my heritage again." The realtor looks out the window for a few moments and I sit, wordless, waiting.

Finally he looks back at me and speaks.

"I am Abenaki, one of 'The People' as they like to call us. And do you know what that's done for me? Caused a wealth of problems, stigmas and prejudices over the years. I am more than just an Indian, Mrs. Solomon, something that you can't understand. But we're not here to discuss my native roots are we?" He goes on without waiting for a reply. "You want to know about the homes at Hawthorne Estates? I'll tell you all I know, for the next five minutes that is," Cy glances at an expensive looking watch.

"Certainly," I say, guilt building in my chest. What right have I to barge in on this stranger, ask nosy questions about his lineage? But then I think of the newspaper article and the knife in my wall. I need answers.

"Can you tell me about the process itself when the homes were built? It seems," I pause, searching for the right word, "unusual that one realtor would handle the entire development."

Cy shrugs, his perfectly starched blue shirt wrinkling momentarily.

"Not really. James Smith and I had a great professional relationship. When I heard that the houses were in the development stage, we worked together on selling them. Not very unusual from a business perspective."

"Do you still do work with him?"

"He's retired."

"And what about the homeowners themselves? Is there anything you noticed as unusual about them as a whole?"

"Unusual? What do you mean?"

Cy crosses his arms over his chest and leans back slightly in his chair.

"I don't know. It just seems odd to me that every home sold more than twenty years ago has never gone up for sale again. Isn't that a bit strange? And the people themselves, they seem. . ." I break off, uncertain.

"Seem what?"

I look out the windows myself now, collecting my thoughts, thinking through my words before I say them.

"Closed off, I suppose. Unfriendly."

Cy laughs, an easy sound that tells me he has lots of practice.

"Mrs. Solomon, Sarah. May I call you that?" I nod. "This is New England, Sarah. Vermont in particular is known for breeding a special sort of people, those eccentric enough or stalwartly enough to settle here aren't known for their outgoingness."

I force a smile.

"I know. But this isn't just unfriendliness, it's more, I don't know . . . hostile."

"Xenophobia, perhaps," Cy smiles again. "You're familiar with the term?"

I nod, but he goes on without pause.

"Fear of outsiders, of strangers." He says the last word slowly, looking me straight in the eye. For some unknown reason, I feel a deep, hot shame. I gather the papers off the small, perfectly polished table and stand.

"Thank you for your time." My words sound stiff, hollow in my own ears.

"Let me walk you out," Cy says, standing from the club chair.

"No, really it's fine. I've wasted enough of your time already." I hurry to the door, not prepared for the weight of it and worry for an instant that my clammy hand won't be able to manage the knob. But I do, and it swings open, and I find myself seconds later outside the tall building sucking in fresh air like a fish tossed back into water.

I don't look up at the tall window where Cy St. Francis watches my retreat. I never see him extract a cell phone from his pocket or hear the words, three stories up, that he says into the phone. But I feel, rather than see, his smoldering dark eyes following my car's path out of the parking lot and back onto the highway.

{Chapter Twenty-three}

Moths flutter in my belly, an uncomfortable, unsettled feeling making it impossible to relax. I pour myself a glass of Merlot, drink it down like juice and then pour another. The tall stem of the glass trembles in my fingers as warmth spreads outward from my stomach. *Just tonight. A little something to dull the edges.*

I spread the paperwork before the fireplace and press a button to light it. The gas insert worried me the first few times I used it, but now it's hard to imagine living without it. The fireplace is one of the very few things that makes the house feel anything like a home to me; well, that and the glass of wine in my hand. I take another sip and lean back against the leather couch. Flames send dancing shadows on the walls, heat spreading in a semi-circle in front of the hearth.

The paperwork holds no interest for me. I try to read it again, but what's the point? I know everything there is to know about my neighbors now, on paper at least. I know which person goes with which house number and who holds the deed. I know when they moved in and, in some cases, where they moved from. But what does any of it matter?

The amount I don't know is so much greater: why the enmity, what Charlotte and Andrew and the other man were doing in the woods and what was in that bag. . .

I wake suddenly, heart racing. The firelight is even brighter now, flames high and licking the panes of glass they're trapped behind. What woke me? A sound.

I listen, heartbeat banging noisily in my ears. The glass in my hand is tipped sideways, the tiny amount of wine left in the bottom, ruby in the light. I set it soundlessly on an end table and move into a crouch. My legs are prickly, and I long to stretch up and relieve the feeling but stay where I am.

Seconds pass.

Nothing.

A minute, two.

Finally, I give up and prepare to stretch to my full height. But then I hear it again.

A noise toward the rear of the house. A slow scratching followed by a quick tap.

Tree branches, it must be. I comfort myself with this thought as I move stealthily toward the direction of the noise. Peeking out a nearby window, I see nothing. The moonlit night is motionless, silent. Stars above prick the velvet sky like tiny, fiery darts.

I'm halfway down the hallway along the back of the house when I hear the noise again. This time the scratch is louder. I bash my foot into the doorframe of the bathroom and let out a cry. I crouch again, listening, rubbing my foot which throbs. My tongue is thick and dry, the alcohol leaving an unpleasant sour taste. Toes aching, I suddenly, irrationally feel anger at Cole. Where is he right now? Pictures flood my mind of him on a golf course, or enjoying a six-course dinner in a cozy, warm dining room. Fury rises hot and fast in my chest. Damn him! And damn me for staying here and playing Nancy Drew.

The absurdity of my situation suddenly hits me, and I feel a panicky sort of laugh choke out. Here I sit, a grown woman, slightly buzzed on wine with a foot likely full of sprained toes hiding in the dark because of a sound outdoors.

"For pity's sake, Sarah," my voice is a quiet whisper. "Get your bloody self together and act like a grown up."

I stand, no longer caring about the possibility of whatever or whoever is outside the window seeing me. Then I hobble to the entry way closet, remove a high powered torch and a can of pepper spray and unlock the rear patio door. The sounds were last coming from the western portion of the house.

The air is breezy and cold. I hear the sound of the brook tumbling in the woods nearby, and frogs, despite the chill, peeping low and hoarse. Cold seeps through my socks as I cross the stone patio and hunker low near the pergola. Dead looking vines hide me from the rest of the yard. I move several out of the way with the butt end of the torch, making a peep hole. The yard is quiet other than the brook. I scan the space but see nothing out of the ordinary.

I wait.

Minutes later, feet numb with cold, I hear the noise again. This time the scratch is faint, still from the western part of the house, but further away. It's moving, whatever it is.

I creep along the back of the house staying close to the foundation where the stone is still faintly warm, holding some of the heat from earlier in the day. The torch feels solid in my left hand, the pepper spray held tight in my other.

Rounding the corner of the house, I hunker down behind a large bush. I picture Bevins on the other side of the bush hunkered down just like me. Waiting. Watching. Scratchy green branches poke my bare arms, and I shiver.

I wait one minute.

Two.

Nothing.

A smeary cloud passes over the moon momentarily, and everything around turns black. But when it moves on, sliding across the surface of the sky like an ice skater, I catch my breath. Standing four feet from me on the other side of the bush is a wolf.

The animal is bushy with a long, full tail. He sniffs the air delicately, like a wine connoisseur. Then his hackles raise, and a low rumble begins in his chest. My right hand, still holding the pepper spray and spreading apart the branches of the bush, instantly begins to tremble.

Oh my God.

The wolf isn't looking toward me though, but out toward the woods behind the house. The growl dies away, but his gaze remains on the trees. I breathe as silently as I can, willing myself not to sneeze or lose my grip on the branches. Finally, after what feels like an hour but is probably less than a minute, the wolf bends his head to the ground, picks up a large stick and runs lightly across the grass and into the forest.

The stick. That's what made the scratching sound scraping along the foundation or the siding. Though it was an odd stick, pale and gray with a knobby end. Smooth as . . . no, it can't be.

I put the thought out of my head, retrace my steps to the patio, looking behind me and to every side all the way. I see the wolf jumping out in front of me, white grin, teeth flashing. I imagine him rushing at me from behind, jumping, claws and fangs . . . and then I'm inside the door and press myself against it, shaking and cold and thanking God for bringing me safely back into this horrible crypt of a house.

It isn't until after a very long and very hot shower, not until I'm tucked into bed with a mountain of blankets and pillows and pepper spray on my bedside table, that I let myself think again about the stick in the wolf's mouth.

Not a stick.

A bone.

{Chapter Twenty-four}

"A wolf? Not likely in these parts, Sarah." John Running Bear's hands are clasped over his sizable belly, his head leaning forward in a way that makes me know he's taking me seriously.

"No wolves in Vermont for years. Last one was shot up at Hard'ack, the big hill in St. Albans. There's a monument there; I guess at the time it was something to celebrate."

"What then? It wasn't a dog."

"Nope, likely not. I believe it was a wild animal like you said, just not a wolf. Probably its cousin, the coyote."

"Aren't they pretty small? And shy? They," I correct myself, "it wouldn't come so close to my house, would it?"

"Well, now, that's a good question. Coyote, coy dogs we call 'em around here, they're not so shy anymore. Been adapting over the years, becoming more familiar with people. I saw a documentary on them a couple of months ago, hundreds of them are living in metropolitan areas. All over the cities you see them out at night crossing the main drags, pilfering garbage cans. Even their size has changed, some of them breeding with wolves. Course, that's not common around here."

"But aren't they pack animals?"

"Not like wolves. They have family units but they don't hunt like wolves with a hierarchy and alpha male and all that. They have their territories and maintain a perimeter, more like a lion in the savannah. Except they've only got one female, not a pride of them. Speaking of which," John smiles slow, eyes crinkling at the corners. "How's that husband of yours?"

I say nothing, roll my eyes.

"Not ready to run away with me yet?"

"Oh, so tempting," I say. "But what about this coy dog? Where did it get that. . ." I stammer.

"Bone?" John fills in. "How big was it?"

I show him with my hands.

"Could have been a deer bone, cow bone maybe."

"There are cow bones just out lying around? I mean, I could see a deer bone if one was killed in the woods. But a domestic animal?"

"Sometimes. Farmers used to take a different approach to putting animals down in the old days. Didn't bother with a veterinarian, just shot the poor thing in the woods, left it there."

"That's disgusting!"

John shrugs. "Got the job done. I bet the poor, sick cow didn't care much at that point how it died, long as it was quick."

John took a sip of his soda, offered me a drink again which I declined.

"So, what else you got for me? One thing you've gotta understand about me, Sarah, is that I'm an honorary Hardy Boy. There's no mystery that I can't solve." He takes another sip from his can, a smile spreading over his tan face. "With enough clues, that is."

I fill him in on recent events, leaving out the paper I found fluttering on the holly bush, just as I did with Grace. I tell him instead about my visit with Cy St. Francis.

John rolls his eyes and makes a "pshaw" sound at the mention of the man.

"That pretty boy? A traitor to his kind."

"How so?"

John looks past me, out the front window. His expression grows serious, lines creasing his otherwise happy face.

"Selling off the houses in that snooty. . ." he catches himself. "Sorry. I don't mean any offense."

"None taken."

"That land was Abenaki property, and he weaseled his way into that deal with Smith and then weaseled his way into hefty profits from selling off his own kin's property. And it wasn't the only time he screwed us over," John's voice is rising, his eyes hooded and dark.

"The elders would have shunned him in the old days. The rest of us do now, not that he notices or cares. It's easy to forget about your guilt nowadays. You just leave town, start a new life in a rich town miles away and reap all the benefits of your greed."

I let a moment of silence pass before I ask the next question. I don't want to insult John. He's one of only two friends I have, and I need both desperately.

"But it's not declared Abenaki land officially, is it?"

John sits silent a moment, eyes hard. But when he looks at me his face softens.

"That's not the way it works around here, Sarah. Not for The People. Not for a long time, if ever. The official White government makes sure that we aren't recognized as an Indian tribe. That way they don't have to give us anything and they can take what they want. Are they the only ones to blame? Probably not. We're not the most organized tribe in the U.S., so you're right in a way. That land isn't ours on paper. And paper," he takes another swig of soda, "is what matters."

A few minutes pass in silence as we study the fire in the potbelly stove. The flames lick and dance.

"So, what's next?" John breaks the silence.

"I'm not quite sure. Research, I guess. I want to look for the family that left, the ones whose home burned down. After that," I shrug, "I'm not sure what else I can do."

"Well, let me know if I can help you with anything."

Silence for another minute as we watch the flames again.

"There is something, actually," I say. "Do you think you could arrange a meeting between me and the elders that were at Hawthorne Estates protesting against Smith?"

John frowns.

"Well, that'll be tricky. Only one left. Henry Lampman is dead, heart attack three years ago. Not sure about George St. Francis, and no, before you ask, he's not a direct relation of Cy. Think he might be in a nursing home. I'll check. The woman though, she'll be impossible to find."

"Why's that?"

"Her daughter died when she was a toddler. After that the woman went bonkers. She was old to be a first-time mama, early forties. Some people say that's why the baby wasn't healthy. Not sure about that, but something in the woman snapped afterward, you know?"

I nod, sympathetically.

"What was her name?"

"It was Josie. Josie Little Fish."

The room starts to wobble around me.

"Sarah, you OK?"

"What? Yes, I'm fine. I think I'll take that drink now though, if you don't mind."

John moves behind the counter, retrieving a V-8 from the small fridge and pouring it into a plastic tumbler for me. His eyes never leave my face which I'm sure is pure white.

"Josie Little Fish? I saw her at the Historical Museum. Or rather, a wax figure of her."

John nods, hands the drink to me. The cold glass feels good in my hand. Centering. I take a sip and then a slow, deep breath. If only there was vodka in it.

"Yeah, they had done those figures of two of the council members. I guess they never got around to poor Henry. It was some project by a local artist with some grant money. "Get in touch with your inner Indian," or some such foolishness. It was a long time ago—they've held up well—must have been made twenty years ago. Maybe more."

"So that's Josie. The woman from the council who protested?"

John nodded.

"And she's the one who went. . ." my voice drifts off, then reappears. "The one who lost her daughter. She went incognito?"

"That's a nice way to put it. Went nuts is more like it. But who could blame her? Losing a kid," John shakes his head, wrinkles creasing his baby-smooth forehead. "Worse than death, I'd imagine. Especially since it was her fault."

I sit straighter in my chair.

"How so?"

"Well, Sarah, you're about to hear just one more reason to dislike Cy St. Francis. His dad, really, but it's hard not to see the old man in the son, you know?" John continues without waiting for a reply.

"Josie and Ike St. Francis, they were a couple. Never married, but they lived together for years. He was a big drinker, into heavier stuff some people say. Ike was a manipulative bastard," John's voice cuts out quickly. "Excuse my French."

I nod at him to continue.

"Anyway, they had all kinds of marital problems, minus the marriage part. She'd leave him, then come back, leave again, then come back. No one knew what she saw in him other than his looks. Once when she left she came back pregnant. We heard that he beat her up pretty badly then. Maybe that's why the baby wasn't, well, normal. But the night Josie's daughter died, Ike had been partying hard, I guess. Came home late, beat the crap out of Josie and then passed out at some point. When she came to, it was mid-day. Elaina Rose, that was the little girl's name, she'd somehow gotten out of her crib. Went out the front door and kept walking. It was freezing cold, middle of winter."

John's voice drifts off as he stares out the windows at the front of the office.

"Nobody knows why the little girl did it, where she was going. Maybe she found her mother unconscious and was trying to find help. Who knows?" His eyes are sad, voice low and deep and filled with sorrow.

"They found Elaina's body the next day, half-covered in snow. Josie went bat shit as you can imagine. Tried to tear Ike's eyes out. She wasn't ever the same after that. Something inside her broke, died that day."

"And you don't know where she is now?"

"Nobody does. Before the police investigation she vanished. Poof," John motions with his fingers like a mini-explosion. "Just gone. Some people say she lives in the woods, like the old days. That she's made herself a lodge up in the hills, hunts and gathers food. Others say she threw herself off Brandon's Bridge or put rocks in her pockets and waded into Fairfield Pond. No body was ever found, though the local police force didn't drag every body of water in the state. Who knows? She could be in a psych ward in New York City for all any of us know."

A heavy sadness rests in my stomach as I set the empty glass onto the small card table, thank John for his time. What must that poor woman have felt? I see her now, standing near the edge of the tree line, face immobile. Cast in stone.

John follows me to the door, leaning against the frame as I go out.

"I'll check on George St. Francis. See if I can find anything out about him. Not sure of his memory, might have dementia by now. He was the oldest of the three."

"Thank you," I say. "Thanks for helping me with all this."

"My pleasure, Sarah. And remember," his eyes start to laugh before his mouth, "if you ever need a break from that husband of yours, come see the Running Bear."

{Chapter Twenty-five}

The evening is turning into night. Stars begin to poke through the sky above, anemic white in the still blue sky. I button my sweater and hop into the car, feeling guilty for driving the short distance from the Abenkaki center to my next stop but too cold to force myself to walk. The Franklin County Free Library is brightly lit. A few people mill around the tall shelves of books; a little boy stands at the bank of windows, face pressed to the glass.

The email address Alicia Gray gave me for Rebecca came back as undeliverable. Intentional? I don't doubt it. I tracked down the phone number for some Rainville's in Hinesburg and left a message but haven't heard back. Maybe I'll uncover something more tonight and maybe there will be a voicemail waiting for me from Rebecca later tonight. Maybe.

The library door creaks when it opens. The same young woman with the nose ring and matted hair is working behind the desk. The mats are now forming into loose dreadlocks, and she's woven chunky beads and bits of colorful thread into some of them.

"CanIhelpyou?" She speaks fast, blurring her words so that they sound like a single long one. A canned energy drink sits on the desk, and she takes a final swig before tossing it into the recycle bin.

"Yes. I was here a few. . . "

She interrupts, "The Brit. I remember now. Microfiche. You wanna look for something else?"

"Yes. I want to find out more about the house fire that happened at Hawthorne Estates, but there wasn't a great deal mentioned in the archives I was looking at. Would there be other area newspapers on film that I could research?"

I notice a movement to my right, a face hidden behind a copy of the *Burlington Gazette*. A man's hand flicks the corner smartly.

"Absolutely," the woman says drawing my attention back. She comes through the half door, which swings behind her like she's exiting a saloon. "Right this way."

I hear a slight hum coming from behind the newspaper. Not a tune, but a short, low noise.

"Coming?" Ms. Dreadlocks stands at the basement door, holding it open. An ugly green dress, made from some wrinkly fabric, gathers around her calves. Her feet are hidden in heavy-soled combat boots, the laces purple and white.

"Sorry, yes." I follow her down the steep steps, and we go through the same process as before. This time it's an abbreviated lesson for me. She leaves me amid a stack of boxes each containing film from different newspapers in Vermont.

"Youokayhere?" The energy drink must be kicking in. Her fingers twitch over her dreadlocks, playing with beads, twirling sections. She's smiling at me but tapping her foot impatiently.

"Fine. Thank you for your help."

She shrugs, nods, and hurries back to the closed door leading to the floor above.

"We close in forty minutes," she says over her shoulder.

"Thanks."

Though the local paper didn't have much coverage, I find a lengthy section in the newspaper of a neighboring town. I enlarge the page, adjust the margins and send it to the printer nearby. The noise of the printing paper is nearly lost over the loud drone of the old dinosaur. The process is time consuming at best, boring as hell at worst, but the documents will come in handy. Search, scan, send to printer. It's easier now that I have the date. Another article, shorter, gets sent to the printing queue. I keep looking.

I've just printed a fourth article and am replacing the roll of film carefully in its battered cardboard box when the basement plunges into darkness. The light from the microfiche machine ekes out a dim gray halo, and a red exit lights glows across the long hallway. Squiggles of light dance before my eyes as they slowly adjust. I swallow once, twice, my fingers smoothing the soft cardboard box.

"Hello?" I call.

No answer.

I clear my throat and turn the microfiche machine off completely so that I can hear over its loud hum. The room quiets to near silence, just a slight trickle of water moving through some pipes overhead. I grab at my handbag searching blindly for my cell. Then I remember seeing it on the kitchen counter, charging, before I left.

"Excuse me!" I call, louder, voice ricocheting off the concrete walls. "Can you please turn the lights back on?"

In response a vacuum cleaner starts above me, growling across the floor.

Damn.

I set the cardboard box into the larger storage cube near the molded chair where I was sitting and fumble my way towards the exit sign. The air is cool and dry on my outstretched hands. I hold them in front of me, a slow game of blind man's bluff. Shuffle, shuffle, pause. I keep moving toward the glowing exit sign. My right hip bumps into something hard. I feel around with my hands and realize it's the corner of a bookshelf. There must be a light switch somewhere. Near the stairs, I assume. Hands out in front again, I position myself further into what I think is the aisle. What went where, furniture-wise? I try to remember where tables are positioned, where the large glass vase and half-dead flowers were.

About two yards away from the door, I hear a noise.

Slap. Slap. Slap.

Feet.

Moving my way.

Quickly.

For an instant I feel relief. The librarian has found me. Then the growl of the vacuum cleaner overhead reminds me that she's otherwise occupied. I think of the man sitting behind the newspaper upstairs, the strange tune he was humming, and shiver.

I move left, find a small alcove created by books stacked in high columns. My back presses into something hard and metal. A water fountain?

More steps, loud but slowing.

My breathing is too loud.

I shrink into the space between the books, crouching a little lower, praying the pile won't suddenly fall to the floor. I remember a cartoon once that depicted a small lion hunter suddenly exposed when all the tall grass around him was flattened by a strong wind. The cartoon man stood, grinning, hiding the spear behind his back while a huge, angry lion approached.

"I know you're in here," a man's voice says loudly enough to be heard over the vacuum overhead. Then the strange humming begins again, a tune I can't place, broken a second later by a low chuckle.

He's close. Too close to me. I press back harder, the metal knob of the fountain digging into my spine. *Stupid place to hide, no place to run.*

The voice comes again from the direction of the only exit. *Should I look for another way out?* I almost laugh, hysterical giggles trapped behind my teeth.

I press my fingers against my lips, hard, and move in small increments trying to see over the tall stack of books. Up, up. Out of the crouch and into a standing position. Then onto tiptoe. But my body wavers and balance wobbles. I start to tip sideways. Hand goes out instinctively. Books fall to the floor in a giant crash, but I catch myself before tumbling after them. Crouching low, I run toward the exit. My purse falls from my shoulder but stays in the hook of my elbow as I run, weaving.

The light from the sign illuminates this part of the room slightly. Almost there. Then a hand reaches out from a blackened corner. I scream, but hard fingers and palm press tight over my mouth. For a moment everything starts to close in around my line of vision. *No. I cannot pass out.*

Fear scrapes up my chest from my belly, cold and sharp.

"I guess you didn't get the message." The voice is low, hard. "Stop poking your nose where it doesn't belong, Mrs. Solomon. Leave the Estates alone."

The man holding the newspaper upstairs. I didn't see his face and can't now. But I think I know whose voice this is. The fear has dislodged something else. Anger, raw and hot.

I have only one chance.

The hand loosens momentarily over my mouth, and I go slack, sink backward into the frame of the man holding me up. He grunts at the change in the weight he's holding, takes a step backward. His grip automatically loosens as he tries to readjust himself in relation to my body weight.

I loosen further, and he nearly staggers as I slump to the left. Then, fueled by adrenaline and rage, I gather all the heat in my belly and jab backward with my right elbow.

It's a hard hit. I can tell by the way the breath whooshes out of his chest, by the grunt in his throat near my ear and by the pain radiating through my wrist and palm. Turning, I plant a knee to his groin. He doubles over, the grunt replaced by a low moan.

"Leave me alone," I yell, voice wobbling with fear. Then I race to the door, purse banging against my hip, shouldering through, up the stairs, tripping once, catching myself on the banister. I run out of the door, the librarian nowhere in sight.

It's not until I'm in my car, doors locked, that I stop to assess damages. My reflection in the thin swath of rearview mirror shows faint red marks near my mouth and jaw line where the strong hand gripped me. Not enough to bruise, though. My hands shake as I push my wild tangle of hair back into its clip.

A smile forms on my lips, and instead of fear, a self-satisfied glow tingles my chest. For the first time in my life I did what a proper heroine in a movie or book should do. Fought off the bad guy, got away. A great weight lifts from my shoulders.

I'm not a victim anymore! I want to scream the words out of my car. Better yet, stand on top of it and yell for all the world to hear. Instead, I satisfy myself with a few more minutes sitting in the silence of my car listening to my breathing slow and my heart rate return to normal. The fissure of pleasure remains, though, and I enjoy every moment of it.

Traffic along Route 7 is slow and erratic. Lights from passing vehicles bathe the nearby trees and sidewalk to the tall brick building. I sit in the parked car twenty minutes. Thirty. He has to come out, and I'm going to wait here until he does.

Several more minutes pass before, finally, the door opens. I lean forward, careful not to press on the horn. The light is dim now, streetlights glowing dull. But it's the librarian who turns, locks the door behind her. Pulls the handle to double check.

I picture him lying unconscious in the basement but know that my blow wasn't hard enough to do that. I wait another fifteen minutes, then back the Lexus onto the road, ready to circle the building. A car bears down on me suddenly, cresting the hill, light shining bright in my mirror. High beams. I hear a rev of an engine and nearly scream. But then they pull around me, pass too fast. Teens, a car full, laughing and talking.

I let out a breath I didn't know I was holding and make the turn to continue my slow circle around the building.

There. The back of the building shows a fire escape. Below it, a line of uniform basement windows. Except one is not the same as the others.

It's open and empty.

{Chapter Twenty-six}

The ringing on the other end of the line seems to last forever. I wish I still had the old-fashioned kind of phone, with the springy, curling cord that I could wind around my fingers. Instead I pace. Walking back and forth between the kitchen nook and the fireplace in the great room, counting.

Four. Five. Six. By the seventh ring I've given up hope of voicemail and am about to disconnect when the ringing stops abruptly.

"Hello?" A woman's voice, out of breath. Youngish. I picture blonde, shoulder length hair and thick bangs, blue eyes.

"Mrs. Rainville? Rebecca? My name is Sarah Solomon. I spoke with your sister. . . "

The voice interrupts me. "Yes, she told me. Said I might hear from you."

"She didn't give me your phone number. The email I sent came back as undeliverable." Why I'm defending the pale gray woman, I have no idea. "I did a little searching online."

Rebecca laughs and even that sounds breathless. "I know. Getting my phone number from Alicia means you'd have to be part of the secret service. She's not exactly the most open person. You aren't, are you?"

There's a smile in her voice, and I like her already.

"No, not part of the secret service."

"Thank God." Her breathing is still erratic. "Sorry, I'm on the exercise bike. Training for an upcoming race, and the freaking rain won't stop."

I glance out my window, but the sky here is pale blue, white clouds stretched like gauze.

"Well, I don't want to keep you. My husband and I bought a house at Hawthorne Estates recently and, well, I wondered if I could treat you to lunch. I just have a few questions. . ."

Rebecca snorts.

"A few? Living in Crazyville, I bet you've got more than a few."

My lips turn up. Yes, I like Rebecca.

"I'm not imagining things then?"

"Doubt it." Her breathing is increasing. "Sorry. Hill repeats." A pause while she guzzles water or a sports drink, then she's back on the line. "I actually only answered because I thought it might be my son. He wasn't feeling very well this morning, but it could be the math test he forgot to study for. Anyway, I can meet you later today if you want, barring getting an SOS from him. I have a client meeting in Burlington, but it should be done by one."

"That would be great. Thanks so much."

We make plans to meet at Ri Ra's, an Irish pub on Church Street at quarter past.

"Thanks so much," I say as we go through the polite goodbyes. "I really appreciate it."

"No problem," says Rebecca. Her breathing is picking up yet again. "Ugh," she pants. "This hill is a mother. See you this afternoon."

I wander Church Street for an hour before our meeting. The sights and sounds here remind me of home. In London, the parks this time of year are filled with flowers of every kind, blossoms drifting down like snow from the trees.

It's still too early here for flowers to bloom, but other smells fill the air on this cobblestone street in the heart of Burlington. Brave diners sitting at outdoor café tables, bundled in woolen sweaters and pea coats, tuck into salads and thick steaks with crusty edges, toasted rolls with warm, soft centers. As I pass by Lake Champlain Chocolates, the seductive scent of warm cocoa meanders out into the street sidling up along innocent pedestrians walking past. My stomach growls.

I sit for several minutes on a park bench and watch people move around me. Sunshine has brought winter-starved individuals gasping from their dark apartments and offices to drink in the liquid gold. The entire street is full of people: businessmen and women in dark suits nodding into cell phones, groups of teenagers and twenty-somethings with pink and green and purple hair spiked into points, dogs practically skipping on the ends of their leashes and tired mothers chasing screeching children.

The sun is intoxicating. I sit and bask in it, face upturned. A guitarist strums a battered looking instrument and sings along, an empty case near his feet. I get so caught up in people watching that I have to jog the last block to make it to the pub on time.

Another wave of homesickness hits me as I stand in the foyer, letting my eyes adjust to the dark interior. I smell fish and chips and see the bartender pulling pints at the wide, shiny bar. Stained glass partitions provide some privacy but only near the front of the pub. The rest is open, tables tucked in against walls and banisters forming a maze that wait staff buzz through like bees.

"Just one?" A pretty redhead asks. A tiny diamond sparkles in her nose, and her smile is toothpaste-white.

"I'm meeting someone actually," I say. Why didn't I think to ask Rebecca what she looked like?

But a woman in a nearby group turns toward me.

"Are you Sarah?" She is tall and willow thin, her dark hair short and shiny. I nod, and she excuses herself from the group.

"Rebecca," she says, and we shake hands. She nods toward the group behind her. "Previous clients," she says over her shoulder as we follow our hostess to a booth overlooking the city park near the rear of the building.

"Thank you very much for meeting me," I say as we slide in.

"Not a problem. Beautiful day, isn't it?"

"Absolutely gorgeous."

"It was raining hard this morning in Hinesburg; that's where we're living now. I usually bike in any weather. You never know what it's going to be like on race day after all. But this morning I just couldn't do it," Rebecca puffs air out of her cheeks, "so I rode the exercise bike. And it sucked. And reminded me why I usually ride in the rain." She laughs then, and I notice that her eyes are as dark as her hair. She looks nothing like her older sister.

"What race are you training for?"

185

"A Century Ride in the Adirondacks. It's a Team in Training race; ever heard of them?"

I shake my head. We order drinks, and she tells me about the organization, which partners willing amateur athletes with patients struggling with lymphoma or leukemia. "We raise money to go toward research. It's good for me. I need a cause, a reason to race otherwise I'm lazy."

I doubt this but smile as she laughs again.

"But enough about me. We're here to discuss Hell Hole Estates, aren't we?" Rebecca takes a sip of her diet Coke and looks out at the park. Her smile fades and her face looks, just for a moment, as gray as her sister's. But then the light outside the window changes, and she is vibrant and pink-cheeked once again. She shakes her head.

"We never should have moved there. And leaving was the best thing we ever did."

"Because of the neighbors?"

Rebecca barks a laugh, a surprisingly rough sound coming from such a pretty face.

"Sorry, but it's hard for me to think of those people as neighbors. Predators, yes. Vultures. But I'm getting ahead of myself, aren't I?" Another sip of soda. "I'll start at the beginning, but this'll be a condensed version." Rebecca looks at her watch, slim like the arm beneath it. "I have to meet with another client at two-thirty."

I nod, leaning forward, and she begins.

"We moved to Hawthorne Estates twelve years ago, when my eldest was just a baby. It was still a fairly new development then, and as far as I know, is still the only gated community in Franklin

County. My husband, Kyle, is involved in politics. At one point he was considering running for governor. Anyway, at that point in our lives, privacy and security were especially important to us.

"Little did we know," Rebecca says, a mirthless smile pulling her lips.

"What?" I ask.

Rebecca looks at me, eyebrows raised. Then she leans forward and says something that sends goose bumps skittering over my arms like ants.

"That our neighbors would try to kill us."

{Chapter Twenty-seven}

"Kill you?" My voice is unreasonably loud in my own ears. A blonde woman with glasses at the table next to us glances in our direction.

"Sorry," I say, voice lower.

"The fire," Rebecca says, re-arranging her silverware. "It was arson. Never proved of course, but we knew."

Arson. I sit for a minute in silence.

Then, "Why was it never proved?"

Rebecca shrugs, her square shoulders rising and falling beneath the thin jacket.

"There was an investigation, if you can call it that. Bevins is in cahoots with some higher-ups in state offices. Police, too, maybe. We didn't push too hard, just wanted to collect the insurance money and get out of there.

"A lot of people in Kyle's family have ostracized us because of it. His family sees things in black and white: we were wronged and should seek and obtain justice. But we don't. See it that way, I mean," Rebecca's voice quiets, and I lean forward to hear the words trailing from her barely opened lips.

"We know what they are, the people in that community, and were happy that all we lost was a house. Things can be replaced. My kids, my husband, can't."

I sit back in my chair. All the air and energy has evaporated from my body. I feel like a hot air balloon just stuck through with an extra-large pin.

A twenty-year old waiter sidles up to the table, tells us about the daily specials. I point to something on the menu, smile weakly as the guy tells me what a good choice I made. Rebecca, on the other hand, is unfazed. She orders a hamburger with fries, extra coleslaw, "It's delicious," she says, and another diet Coke.

Then the waiter is gone.

"I'm sorry, it's a lot to dump on you all at once," Rebecca says, noticing my apparent paralysis. "But you must have suspected something. I mean, otherwise, why get in touch with me?"

I shake myself, mentally, then sip my water, wishing for a stout, dark ale.

"Of course, yes, I did. I knew that something . . . that something wasn't right. My husband, Cole, he's away on business a lot, so it's just been me at the house a lot of the time. The whole neighborhood just feels, I don't know. Off to me." My voice trails away as images fill my head. Andrew Bevins, the knife, photocopies of me tied to the holly, strong hands over my mouth in the basement of the library. And the woman, the ghost, I've seen more than once.

I ask Rebecca if she's ever seen anyone matching that description. She shakes her head. "I saw some weird stuff up there, but no, not an old woman in the woods. Who knows? Maybe they conjured her to life."

I smile, but a tremble passes through my body.

"What did you mean, 'we know what they are.' What are they?"

Rebecca frowns then lets out a sigh. She looks out the window again, and I see lines across her forehead and at the corners of her eyes that I hadn't noticed.

"Some sort of cult. Satanism is a word you don't hear a lot these days, but I've often wondered if that's what it's related to. I didn't get to the bottom of it but something to do with the dark arts if you want to call it that."

I want to laugh. Inside a giggle is bubbling like the top of a bottle of champagne ready to spew. This whole thing is bloody ridiculous. Here I sit with a stranger discussing my neighbors who are in a cult. Is this real? I swallow, and the hysterical laughter subsides.

"What am I going to do?" I ask out loud, not really questioning Rebecca but the world in general.

"Move. Get out of there. Believe me, Sarah, you'll be better off. Happier. Healthier. You'll get your safety back and more important, your sanity."

I start to cry then, embarrassed beyond belief as slow, salty rivers cover my cheeks. I press the thick white napkin into my face. Rebecca sits across from me frozen like a deer in oncoming traffic.

"I'm sorry. This is really quite humiliating," I wipe the tears away hard, wondering if black mascara trails are left behind.

"It's OK," she says but still looks uncomfortable. Who can blame her? Strange English woman sobbing into her lunch.

"It's just that. . . " I pause, take in a deep, shaky breath. "It's just that part of me wondered if I was crazy, if I had in fact lost touch with sanity. And these actually are tears of relief," I laugh. "It feels incredibly good to know that I'm not nuts, that you experienced these things too. Not that I'm glad you did, you understand, it's just. . . "

Rebecca interrupts me, places a cool hand on my arm. Her eyes are chocolate covered and so dark it's hard to make out her pupils.

"I know."

We discuss other things while we eat. Apparently, I ordered a grilled vegetable sandwich which I don't remember asking for but which tastes delicious. The bread is lightly toasted, glossed with butter and the vegetables are fresh and perfectly sautéed. A thick layer of garlic pesto lines the bread. The fries are hand-cut, thick and salty, and the ale, which I remembered to ask for when the waiter returned, contrasts them perfectly. Rebecca digs heartily into her meal wiping her fingers on the napkin and groaning in pleasure.

"This is the best thing about training," she says, popping another French fry into her mouth.

I smile, and we chat about other things, Rebecca's kids and my life growing up in England. It turns out that Rebecca spent a semester there in college so we compare notes on favorite shops and restaurants. Finally, we push our plates away. I use the ladies room, and when I return, Rebecca is consulting her watch.

"I have to go," she says, picking up the bill in a tanned hand. "My treat."

I start to argue with her, but she shakes her head, pulls me into a teepee hug, our shoulders grazing.

"Don't forget what I said," she says close to my ear. "It's not worth it. Believe me."

We let go of each other, and for a moment I feel dizzy, disconnected. I put a hand on the back of my chair.

"Thank you. For everything."

She smiles, waves and then winds her way to the register.

I sit another few minutes, sipping the rest of my drink which is now warm. My head is starting to hurt slightly. A beautiful, chilly breeze comes through the back windows mingling the scent of baby grass and budding trees with rich food.

What's next? Rebecca's words run in a loop round my head. *Move. Get out of there.* But can I? There are three tiers of obstacles. Cole, first of all. He loves this place and the house and the neighborhood and has seen none of what I have. Secondly, there is the thought that if I give up, give in and get out, this will happen again. Some other woman will be in my place next year or the one after that. I rub my fingers absently over the edge of the tablecloth, noticing a small fray.

The third reason is one that fills me with fire, rekindled every time I think about the things that have happened to me in the past few weeks. This house is not one that I love. The neighbors are strange, maybe even dangerous. The climate is not appealing to a sun-lover like me. But there is a strong cord tightening within me that I recognize. One that I haven't felt in many months, maybe even years. It's not heroic or high-minded. It's just plain old stubbornness.

How dare they try to displace us? Bully me? Come into my private space and scare me? I feel the

192

heat of my anger, rising from belly to breast, and I fan those flames. Because now is not a time to feel fear. It's a time to act, and anger will be the impetus to keep me going. It's about not being a victim anymore; I spent enough time in that role in Philadelphia. I won't go to that dark place again.

If I keep going, if I keep reaching and pushing, I'll get to somewhere I've never been. That's my hope at least, I think, as I stand up and walk out the door.

{Chapter Twenty-eight}

When I pull into the driveway, I'm pleased to see Cole's SUV parked near the stone steps. I squeeze my car by it in the circular drive and park on my side of the garage then go in through the side door. He's speaking in another room as I walk into the kitchen. I follow the sound of his voice, pausing outside the door.

". . . for tonight. OK. Thanks."

I walk into the great room. The gas fire isn't lit, and the room is chilly. I wish again that I'd taken Cole up on the offer of having the rooms painted before we moved in. The light gray walls make me feel even colder.

A manila envelope sits on the Stickley coffee table, and a single sheet of paper lies on the floor. Cole is turned away from me facing the bank of windows on the far side of the room, hands on narrow hips, his shoulders slumped slightly.

"It's good to see you," I say, and my words make him jump. He turns fast, and I see something bad written on his face.

"What is it?" I move across the room, fast, hands outstretched. The great room feels like a football field. As though the faster I move, the farther the goal line is getting.

"Don't you know?" his voice is a harsh bark. I stop, inches from him. Heat radiates from his body under the rumpled suit. His hands are clenched into tight circles at his side.

"Know what?"

His eyes search every centimeter of my face. Inspecting it for what?

"After everything we've been through. . . "

"Cole, you're scaring me. What are you talking about?" My voice trembles, and I steady the rest of myself on the back of the nearest chair. The leather is creamy-soft beneath hands that have grown icy.

"Like you don't know." He spits the words out, hard as pebbles.

"I don't. Why don't you stop talking in riddles, and tell me what's happened?"

Cole passes a hand over his face. The knuckles are red and swollen looking. It's then that I notice the hole in the plaster, gaping. A small pile of white and gray lie on the floor under it like chunks of snow. A lamp nearby, smashed.

"Look in the envelope over there," he nods toward the coffee table. "The contents should refresh your memory."

I retrace my steps, feeling slightly dizzy. Impossibly, the room has grown in length in the moments since I crossed it. Knees shaking, I stoop and pick up the manila envelope. It's creased on one corner. I slide jittery fingertips under the seal, but it's already been opened. Of course, it's been opened.

The envelope wavers slightly in my hands, and then I shake it, and the contents spill out into my empty hand. Photos, clear and glossy. Five in all, each showing a couple talking over a table. I notice the details first. The way the starched white tablecloth makes perfect waterfalls of fabric. The hands of the couple, entwined. One set pale white, the other darkly tanned. Then I move up to their faces. Cy St. Francis, handsome, dark-skinned, bending his face toward the woman. She has dark, curly hair. In one photo her head is thrown back in laughter; in another, his lips are perfectly formed to hers.

"Where did you get these?"

Then before he can answer, "They aren't real, Cole. That's not me. I mean, it is me but I never . . . not with Cy, not. . ."

"There's more." My husband's voice bursts through the bubble making me slow and stupid.

"So that's his name? Looks like quite a catch, Sarah. Handsome guy, isn't he?" He grabs at his shirt collar, pulling. I recognize this gesture. Extreme stress. Overwhelm.

"How long has it been going on?"

"It hasn't. That's what I'm trying to tell you! Look, I know this looks bad, but I swear to you. . ."

Cole barks out a laugh.

"Looks bad? Ah, Sarah. The queen of understatement."

"This isn't me, Cole! It's . . . it's Photoshop or something. I swear I never had dinner with this man. I went to see him in his office in Shelburne. That's all. I was there on business, Cole, not for pleasure. Just ask. . ." my voice trails off. But who could he ask?

"There's more," he says, head dropping into his hands. "Apparently you forgot something at his place. Or maybe it was here, huh, Sarah? You have this big house to yourself while I'm away." His voice is muffled, but I can hear the rage there. And the pain.

He points in the direction of the envelope without lifting his head. My fingers crawl inside again as though by their own will. Because I don't want to know what else is here. Probing, my hand grazes first one side and then the other. Nothing. But then, toward the bottom pushed hard against the seam, fabric. It's small, crushed into a tiny packet. I pull, and it catches once on the back of the metal tab before releasing. Panties. Delicate black lace, sheer. A small piece of white paper is tucked between the folds.

"Did you read this?" My voice is shaking as hard as my hands.

Cole nods without raising his head. I smooth out the creases of the paper, try to breathe.

"Sarah," the letter starts in an unfamiliar hand, "I told you that we have to tell your husband about us. I can't keep this inside any longer. If you won't leave him. . ." My hands, which haven't stopped trembling, suddenly still.

Gray pushes in on my vision then, suffocating. Buzzing in my head. Room around me grows smaller and smaller, until I feel the walls near my elbows and knees. *No, not again.* And then, blessedly, slip into blackness.

"Sarah?" A voice calls me, but I'm under thick blankets, cocooned in warmth. My bedroom is lit with explosions of sunlight, but I burrow deeper into my bed, clenching my eyes.

I smell bacon frying. Mum stands at the hot stove, one hand on hip, the other rearranging fatty pieces of meat on a plate. She's humming, and wisps of hair have unraveled from the messy bun on her head. She turns, and I wait for her smile, the rosy cheeks and the mischievous eyes. But they aren't there.

Instead her face is blank, as though a hand erased every bit of her features. No eyes or cheeks or nose. But still the humming comes, and I realize now, in horror, that it's coming from a mouth that isn't there. That it's not a tune she's singing but words that she can't free, trapped behind lips that are no longer there.

{Chapter Twenty-nine}

I struggle upright, screaming.

"Ma'am, shhhhhh, it's OK."

Wildly, I look around. See the great room, the dull gray walls, and the perfectly placed furniture. My head is pounding as though a woodpecker is drilling a hole over my left ear. I put my hand there and feel a swath of fabric, cotton and thick.

"You took a fall," the voice tells me. "You're OK. We just need you to lie still for a bit longer. They're bringing a stretcher in."

A woman dressed in a blue uniform, a stethoscope around her neck, is kneeling on the floor by my side, smoothing my hair, easing my head back onto the pillow on the plush carpet.

"It's OK, sweetie. Everything is going to be fine."

I moan.

"Is the pain bad?"

I shake my head, no, but then the pain is.

"It's not going to be OK," I whisper. "Never again. He thinks that I. . ."

"Shhhhh, don't try to talk. Just rest until they get the stretcher."

The hospital smells very much like any other hospital I've ever been in: a dry, papery smell, the sharp tinge of alcohol and a slight odor of overcooked food. Medical personnel hurry through the halls, many with charts or laptops in their hands. I've been discharged from the ER, but they want to keep me overnight, just as a precaution.

Cole has been by my side the entire time, but hasn't said a word. Not to me, at least. He answers the doctor's questions calmly, crosses one leg over the other and leans his elbow on a nearby table as we wait for yet another nurse to come and ask yet another series of questions. Perhaps this is the new way of winnowing out the truly emergent cases from the hypochondriacs, I think, as nurse number three scribbles my replies onto a form. Paperwork them into fleeing on foot.

Now, though, my wheelchair glides silently along the corridor and into Room 207. The room is empty, but one of the beds is made up with fresh sheets and a thin, cotton blanket. It's mulberry-colored and faded, probably been washed a hundred times.

The room is quiet, the hallway noise nearly nonexistent, when the heavy door swings shut after the nurse. Cole helps me onto the edge of the bed, though I don't need him to, and starts to untie my shoes. It's then that the tears come, hot and fast. I swipe at my face but more fall in their place. If he notices, my husband doesn't respond.

"Would you like me to get you a nightgown from home?" he asks instead.

"I'll be fine," I say and wipe my face again. A tiny pile of crumpled tissues mounts on the mattress beside me.

"I know you still don't believe me," I begin, but Cole stops me with a hand raised in defeat.

"Please, Sarah. Would you? If the tables were turned, would you? All these trips you haven't wanted to go on. I should have known. . ."

"That has nothing to do with this! It wasn't him, it was, is, this neighborhood. Something really bad is going on here, Cole, and I feel like I'm running to put the pieces of the puzzle together before they're burned up. But Bevins and St. Francis and who knows who else is right behind me! Someone grabbed me at the library, did you know that? Threatened me. Put their hands over my mouth and . . ."

"Sarah. Please, just stop."

"I'm telling you the truth. While you're off on all of these trips, things have been happening here, Cole. You have to believe me. I'm not imagining this or making it up. I swear to you!"

A nurse knocks on the door and comes in without waiting for a reply. She's wearing pink scrubs with orange trim. She looks like a cone of Sherbet, and I'm annoyed that she's here, bothering us, interrupting.

"Sorry, Mrs. Solomon," she says, reading the message on my face. "I just wanted to let you know that we'll have meds for you at the nurses' station in a couple of hours. We have to wait for the swelling to go down a bit before you take anything, but it won't be long now. Can I get you anything? Juice or a glass of water?"

I shake my head, thank her, wait for her to leave.

The room is silent again. Then, "I'm going home, Sarah. I'll be back to pick you up in the morning."

I nod, but the motion makes my head hurt more. Wiping my eyes again, I look at my husband.

For the first time, I see signs of aging—small lines around his eyes and lips, a few gray hairs streaking his temples. His skin is pale.

I say, "thank you," when what I want to do is cling to his hand and beg him not to leave me in this strange place.

I circle the room, then sit on the bed, then lay down. Watching shadows on the wall, I can't stop the flow of recent events from marching around my head one after the other. Giving up on sleep, instead I listen to the foreign sounds outside my door. Beeps, soft footfalls, murmuring voices. I wonder what Cole will do with the photos, with the rest of the contents of the packet. I picture Cy St. Francis buying them at Victoria's Secret. Or was it Bevins? Maybe it was an errand for Charlotte when she was on one of her shopping trips.

My mind drifts back to happier times, times in England which remain sun-filled in my memory. Romping through the countryside, the smells and tastes and sounds that I miss so much. Cole's face, handsome and tanned then, both of us pink-cheeked. We were so happy, took so much pleasure in small things: the slant of the sun on top of a mountain, the way the woods smelled after rain, the sounds of the birds and the heady anticipation when we planned for a new weekend adventure.

Thoughts about my art come next. Sadness sits hard in my chest, a heavy weight. I remember the excitement preparing for the grand opening of the shop. My artwork, made into prints and gift wrap and greeting cards and coasters, each piece splashed with vibrant color. Yet another thing missing in my life now: color. Vermont is gray; our house is gray; my skin feels gray. Perhaps I will metamorphose right into the landscape. Soon, I'll be invisible. Maybe that wouldn't be such a bad thing, being invisible.

A nurse comes in to check my vital signs, asks me if I want something for the pain. I decline, turn on my side and close my eyes. The pounding in my head is uncomfortable, but I welcome it. At least I feel something.

{Chapter Thirty}

The next morning I'm discharged with a diagnosis of mild concussion. I'm told to rest, sleep when I can and let my body do its thing (in more technical terms than this). Another blow to the head in the next several days could be life-threatening. I assure the doctor that I'll be careful, make a joke about wearing my bike helmet around, and then a nurse wheels me through soundless sliding doors into the bright sun. Cole arrives near my elbow, helps me into his SUV. It's a high climb, but his arms are strong, and I get into my seat without falling to the pavement. We wave to the nurse, and he pulls away from the curb.

Silence fills the enclosed space, pressing and hot. The sun feels good on my face, though, and I rest my forehead against the window, watch the houses and shops turn to woods and trees and dense forest as we climb the hill toward Hawthorne Estates. Fatigue settles over my shoulders like a cape. Cole asks if I want anything as we pass the small general store near our road, but I shake my head no.

At home he carries in a duffle bag that he didn't unload after returning from his trip, brings it up to our bedroom. I wander through the rooms downstairs. He's cleaned the blood that I dripped in the great room. The furniture has all been put back in place. There are fresh vacuum tracks in the room, likely from cleaning up the crushed leaves and dirt that the medics' shoes brought into the house. The manila envelope is nowhere in sight.

We spend the rest of the afternoon avoiding one another. He sprawls on the chaise lounge in the great room watching hockey, and I move soundlessly from one room to another trying to settle somewhere but failing. I take a hot bath, but the heat makes my head pound more.

Dinner is stilted. Cole goes out briefly and comes home with Pan Asia takeout which we eat in the great room, he on the lounge again, and I curled up in one of the big wing chairs. I pick at my food, thanking him for going out to get it and put the rest in the fridge. I sip a glass of wine as I put away clean dishes in the kitchen, then a second as I wander upstairs to our bedroom. The closet could be tidied, I think, as I lay across the bed, but I turn my head away instead, staring out the big window. The sun begins its descent toward the horizon, toward the line of mountains to the west. Pale streaks of copper and gold form, then the sun itself turns a delicate shade of red and dips below the mountains. The wine is making me sleepy, but I sit up, rouse myself.

Leaving the glass on the bedside table, I walk to the closet, change into warmer clothes and haul out my hiking boots again. I forgot to remove the mud last time, and small bits of dried dirt fall to the floor of the closet when I move them. Carrying them downstairs, I grab my torch and pepper spray then pause by the back door.

"I'm going for a little walk," I call out. No response.

Cole has fallen asleep, legs and arms at weird angles. The television announcer screams about a player's recent move; leftover dinner is precarious on the glass topped table. Cole looks uncomfortable, but I leave him as he is, move outside. I sit on the still-warm steps, pull on my boots and tie them. Little piles of dirt and leaves remain on the stairs.

The metal gate behind our property squeaks when it closes. I walk along the gravel path. The dimness of the night makes me squint in tree-covered areas like I'm walking through tunnels. Frogs have started their nightly din. The wood frogs make a loud, high trill while the bull frogs *galump-galump* alongside. I let my feet lead me, grateful to just be out of the house away from the undercurrent of anger and pain. Big, deep, breaths ground me. The air smells beautiful, fresh and clean. There's a hint of wood smoke, and the scent adds a tanginess to the cool night. New leaves have popped out on the trees today, buds and tiny green shoots underfoot as well. The sun has worked its magic.

I walk without thinking, concentrating on my breath and the sound the breeze makes as it moves among the branches and needles of the great pine trees. I absorb the sounds and smells, the dimly lit backdrop, letting Mother Nature clean me out. Bands inside my gut loosen. My breathing becomes slow and regular. The thoughts, anxious and swirling throughout this long day, have fallen away, and my only thought is where to place my next foot, what type of amphibian made that sound.

Without thinking, I find myself close to the clearing. Did I intend to come here? The sound of frogs and the occasional flap of wings spread out behind me like a blanket. But in the clearing there will be no sound.

The smell of wood smoke is strong now. For a moment I wonder if someone has snuck into the community, is camping in the woods. I think of the ghost. Perhaps she . . . but then I hear a sound that sends goose bumps up and down my spine. Mumbling voices, then twigs snapping nearby. I hold my breath, then duck low. If I can back onto the path. . . A sound. Directly in front of me and not more than three feet away.

". . . here." a voice says. ". . . the altar. . ."

My left hand covers my mouth. *Not a sound, Sarah. Not a sound.*

Heartbeat loud, I strain to hear over it. There is some shuffling, then one loud grunt and a whoosh of released breath. Another shuffle of feet, branches cracking, leaves crunching. Then, silence.

I see them through the trees, just for an instant, before they are hidden by the large pines pressing close to the clearing. Three people: Bevins, the man with the ski hat, Marc, and Charlotte.

The moon, as though at the group's command, reveals itself once again, pushing clouds away and lighting up the night. Pressing my face as close to the tree line as possible, I still can't quite see them. One of the men speaks, too low for me to hear.

If I can get to the other side of the woods, get closer . . . but doing so will expose me for a few seconds at least, on the walking path in the bright moonlight.

Staying low to the ground, I move to the edge of the trees. If I'm going to do this without getting caught I must be fast and silent, like a deer. I think for an instant of Josie Little Fish and wonder if her feet have walked where mine stand now, if these trees were as familiar to her as they are foreign to me. I wonder if she died out here. I shove the last thought aside and crouch lower, thighs burning.

Deep breath.

Run.

Leaves are nearly soundless under my light footsteps, and I smile wide as I make it to the other tree line, tuck myself in near the largest oak.

My happiness is short-lived. The next step taken, hurried and awkward with tingling legs, results in the loud snap of a branch breaking underfoot. Horrified, my legs tell me to run, run, run. My body is hard and tense, heart loud, breathing stops.

I wait.

"What was that?" It's Charlotte's voice, high and nervous.

For a few moments there is complete silence other than the sound of frogs peeping in some far off swamp. I stay where I am, still as a fencepost.

"Probably a fox. I'll go check it out, though."

I'm not sure which of the two men have spoken. Standing slowly, I press my body into the oak, pull my dark coat sleeves over my hands, dig my beige boots into the leaves underfoot as quietly as possible, hiding anything pale that will stand out in the moonlight like a beacon. My eyes close tight.

Crunching footsteps trail toward the right of me, moving away toward the deeper woods. I open my eyes, exhale low and long. Despite the brightness of the night, I see a torch beam poking through the trees and underbrush. The spring frogs keep up their chorus as the stream of light moves to a stand of trees thirty feet to my right.

Please, please.

The beam of light turns suddenly, making a sharp u-turn. He's coming back. My muscles tense. Footsteps draw closer, the light beam darting in and out of trees close by. Leaves crunch underfoot. How many paces away is he now? Twenty? Fifteen? My breath comes fast, short and noiseless.

I feel, rather than see his presence at first. It's the second man, Marc, his dark coat and hat allowing him to nearly blend in with the tree next to me. We stand parallel to each other. He's facing back, looking out toward the woods. I'm standing straight and still, breath stopped in my throat.

In his left hand is a powerful spotlight, in his right, a gun.

{Chapter Thirty-one}

Marc holds the gun in a familiar way, trained to use it. His elbow is tucked close to his body, eyes shadowed. He's not looking at me but makes a slow circle with the torch, searching the woods beyond where we stand.

Should I move? Crouch further? Try to slide around to the other side of the tree? I do nothing, standing as still as the tree itself, no breath, no blinking. My body is as tense as a rubber band, muscles screaming, adrenaline unleashed. We stand like this for several seconds: he searching the woods and me wishing I were anywhere else in the world.

Finally, after what seems like many hours, he moves abruptly, torch marking his path back to the group. I sag against the tree momentarily.

Thank you thank you thank you.

"I didn't see anything," Marc says.

There is a grunt from Bevins.

"How much longer?" Charlotte asks. Her teeth chatter—rat-a-tat-tat—between words.

"We're just about done," Bevins replies after a few seconds of quiet. ". . . all we need for tomorrow night."

I hear a zipper open, then a scraping sound like something hard being dragged along the leaves. Then the zipper closes again.

". . . already put out the fire." A voice, the second man's, I think.

"Good. Let's go," Bevins says.

I wait for a full five minutes after the last footfall dies away before daring to move from my hiding place. Even then, my actions are as quiet as possible. I slide first one foot then another along the ground, like a skater or ice fisherman testing the strength of the ice underfoot. Easing my way up and away from the tree that supported my weight, I stand, shivering, arms wrapped around my abdomen.

My coat feels made of paper, my fingers numb from holding the metal cylinder of the torch. Stepping slowly at first, then more quickly, I trace the man's steps from my tree to the area where they were huddled.

The clearing is open and empty. Moonlight makes it as bright as early morning. The stone slab is bare. What did one of them call it? *Altar*. I shiver again, then notice something. A dark shape lies near one of the primitive legs of the bench. The oblong shape and width tell me it's similar to or maybe the same heavy duffle bag the two men were carrying the other night.

I move quickly over to it, crouching despite aching leg muscles. Steadying myself on the fingertips of one hand against the earth, I use the other to find the zipper. It is icy, and my already cold fingers are clumsy and heavy.

I pull.

Nothing happens.

I tug again, harder. My fingers slip from the metal piece. Stopping, I bring my fingers up to my mouth, blow on them. They thaw slightly, and I try again.

The third time, the zipper begins to move. Slowly, it inches down, metal teeth releasing. The moonlight disappears completely as a cloud passes over, and for a moment I'm trapped in complete darkness. But the cloud moves on, and the light shines again from above, and my hand has pulled the zipper completely to the other end of the bag. My fingers shake as I part the two sides. My breath stops.

And then a scream catches in my throat. I slap a hand over my mouth, and it turns to a moan.

Pink flesh. The bag is full of pink, hairless flesh. A back. I can't see the arms or legs or the head. I scuttle backward, getting away from the body my only desire. My right foot hits a metal box, and the clanging sound of other metal inside it bashing together shatters the quiet night. I hear the frogs far away and wish I was with them, sitting in the mud, hiding. Safe. My breath comes out in tiny mists of white, and I gulp air and keep moving backward on my hands and feet like some sort of deformed crab.

Twenty feet from the stone table, I stop.

A body. There's a body in that bag. Who? Why? I know what I have to do but everything in me tells me to do the opposite.

Run. Run. Run.

My hands skitter over my jacket searching for my cell phone. Please, let there be a signal. I hold the small silver phone in one hand, but it's shaking so hard I can't make out the signal strength or even the numbers. Slow, steady breaths. *Get yourself under control. You can do this; you will do this.*

Thirty seconds later the phone is ringing. Three minutes later, I've told Cole everything and he's finding shoes as he hangs up. Eighteen minutes later, he crashes through the underbrush, and I put down my torch which I'd used to guide him into the clearing. Can it have taken him such a short time to get to me? It feels as though I've been in the woods for hours now.

"Are you OK?" Cole is rumpled, his shirttail half in and half out of his jeans. His shoes are dirty, caked with mud, and his hair is standing on end. I think that he's never looked better and fall into his arms.

"I'm fine." I say the words but of course, don't mean them. "The police are on their way?"

"They should be here soon," he says, looking at the stone table and the black bag underneath.

"You sure you're OK? I can walk you back to the house. The police can handle this."

"No. I'm fine, just cold. I want to see. . ." my voice trails off. "I want to know what happened."

Cole nods.

We stand huddled together against the cold. His arms around me have never been as welcome.

"Over here!" a voice calls, twenty minutes later. Cole steps back slightly to wave to the officers with his torch, and I feel the cold instantly shimmy into the place where he stood.

There is a crashing of underbrush, and then two officers in dark uniforms with shiny badges emerge. One of them is Chevalier, the officer who came to the house. I'm not sure if I should groan or clap.

Their heavy flashlights are bright on our faces before they drop the beams.

"So, what have we got here?" he asks, approaching us after taking a ten-second look at the stone table.

I fill him in on the night's events: the walk through the forest, the trio, the bag they carried and my exploration of the clearing. And of course, what I found in the bag.

Cole has brought me extra mittens and a hat, and finally my fingers and the tips of my ears are starting to warm.

"Let's have a look, shall we?"

Chevalier moves to the stone slab. The other officer, slight and pale in the moonlight, offers me a nod. He is wearing round glasses and looks as though he'd be more comfortable behind the desk in an accounting office. Not bothering to make introductions, Chevalier leans in close to the bag while the other officer shines a bright torch, illuminating the bag and the ground surrounding it in a pure white beam.

I see the pink flesh again and for a minute imagine vomiting where I stand. Steady, deep breaths as Cole wraps an arm around my shoulders and gives me a gentle squeeze.

Chevalier pulls on latex gloves and slides his hands into the bag, under the body. We wait until, in slow motion, he turns the body, grunting as he slides the top half up and out of the duffle. I picture long, tangled hair or a scarred face—some distinguishing feature that will tell a story about this poor soul.

I'm not at all prepared for what comes out of the bag.

{Chapter Thirty-two}

"Officer Lambert, what do you see here?"

Chevalier calls the question over his shoulder, and the thin, pale partner answers immediately, in monotone.

"I see a porcus, sir. Latin for. . ." his voice hesitates, "pig."

Chevalier stands from his crouched position, the duffle bag split down the middle by a large, pink pig. It lies on its back, dead eyes looking toward the sky as though it's stargazing.

The animal is in perfect condition from where I'm standing, no blood, cuts or wounds that would indicate how it died. This only makes it more unreal, like the pig really is just out for an evening adventure instead of dead, stuffed in a bag and hauled into the forest.

"What is it doing here?" I ask. My question is met by momentary silence.

Chevalier says, "Officer Lambert, check the area."

Lambert nods assent and begins winding his bright torch beam in and around the stone, the duffle, the pig.

"Looks like we won't need to get the coroner out of bed tonight after all," says Chevalier. "As for what it's doing here," the officer looks toward the pig then back to me. "You tell me."

"Hey, wait just a minute. That's not fair," Cole's voice slices cleanly through the fading sound of the frogs and Lambert's crashing around in the undergrowth. Considering his earlier fury toward me, the defensiveness in his voice warms me.

"Are you implying that Sarah had something to do with this?"

"I'm not implying anything," Chevalier's tone makes it quite clear he is. "However, this is the third call we've gotten from Mrs. Solomon in less than two weeks. In each incident, she was alone, no witnesses."

"Well, that's hardly her fault," Cole snaps back. "I'm out of town a lot on business. And if my poor wife can't call the local police department to do its job. . ."

My anger toward Chevalier is exactly matched with my love for my husband.

"We are doing our jobs, sir." Chevalier speaks slowly, clearly. "I'm just stating a few facts, as I see them."

Cole takes a step forward. The veins along his neck strain the skin. I place a hand on his arm.

"Perhaps instead of stating only what you see," I say, my voice trembling, "you could try some creative thinking. Some theories that don't involve me being an attention-seeking drama queen. Or a psychopath." The tremor in my voice is gone.

"For one, there is no way in God's green earth that I could physically haul that," I point to the pig, "through the forest. And why in the world would I want to?"

I take my own step toward the officer but am interrupted by the sound of Lambert's voice.

"Sir? You'll want to take a look at this."

The three of us walk to where the junior officer is kneeling in the leaves near the duffle bag.

A metal container, larger than a lunchbox but with the same old-fashioned handle, sits in front of his knees. It's about two feet in length, narrow and deep. It's dark green or blue, and there is writing on the side, a few scribbled numbers in black sharpie.

"It's an ammo box," Cole says to me.

Chevalier nods, crouching beside the other officer.

"Open it."

Lambert pulls on a heavy-looking metal locking mechanism at the front of the box, and with a springing action, the lock releases. The lid creaks as it opens.

"What the hell. . . "

Cole and I move closer. The contents of the box shimmer in the light from the moon. A sharp, pointed blade. Five white candles, waterproof matches. Salt. And a small packet wrapped in white cloth. The material is common, maybe linen or muslin, found at any craft store. It's folded over and over again, making a lumpy bundle.

"Sir?" Lambert inquires.

"Open it," Chevalier says again.

Lambert moves the cloth slowly away, unfolding and smoothing as he goes. After several lengths of fabric are removed, he uncovers the contents: an antique-looking book. It's battered and worn, probably the size of my hand with fingers spread, brown and soft looking.

"Oh, that's not good." Cole says quietly.

A five-pointed star, faded and black, is the only image on the book's cover. A pentagram. Chevalier gives an abbreviated sigh.

"Wrap it up. Put it all back where it was."

"Yes, sir."

Lambert begins his careful re-wrapping. His movements are slow and precise. Maybe I was wrong thinking he would be more at home in an accountant's office; he might have been a great nurse or doctor.

There's a brief pause.

"What will happen now?" I ask.

"You think you can identify the people who were out here, who carried this in?" Chevalier nods his head toward the stargazing pig.

I nod.

"I'll write up a report. We'll take the pig and the box of," his voice drifts off as he looks behind him at the box, "items," he continues. Then I'll make a visit to your neighbors' houses, see what they have to say."

Cole nods, but I stand, staring at the altar. I'm quiet for several minutes, enough time for Chevalier to notice.

"What is it, Mrs. Solomon?"

Thoughts are swirling in my brain but one sticks out, rough and sharp-edged. Could it work?

"I have an idea," I say.

I spend the next day making a flurry of phone calls. I call Rebecca again to clarify something she said, then a heavy machine company out of Burlington and finally spend a great length of time on the phone being transferred from one desk to another at the Agency of Natural Resources. Annoying elevator music is interrupted periodically by the voice of a man who sounds as though he's just stepped off a movie screen in the 1950s. He tells me about the wealth of information I can now find, conveniently online, by visiting the department's website. Instead, I hold for yet another technician.

Finally, a real person answers on the other end.

"Nate Giroux," says a youngish voice, "ANR, Field Division Office."

I introduce myself, tell him that I'm looking for paperwork dating back to the dig that happened before Smith started the building project.

He whistles through his teeth. I picture him, boots up on an ugly green metal desk, a toothpick sticking out of his mouth.

"That's a ways back, ma'am."

"Yes, I realize that. But this is public record and must be somewhere in your office, right?"

"Not necessarily. It's public record. You're right on that count. But it's doubtful we'd have the paperwork here in our office. In fact, we don't have a lot of paperwork here anymore. Had a flood a few years ago, caused by Hurricane Irene. Most of our documents that were stored in the main facility were ruined."

I grit my teeth. *Perfect.*

"I can check for you though, ma'am."

I thank him, give him my email address, phone number and physical address and ask him to please expedite the search if at all possible.

"I'll do what I can, should be able to let you know within a week or so," Nate says, then says goodbye.

I don't have a week.

{Chapter Thirty-three}

The night air is cold and crisp; temperatures this time of the year still fall well below freezing overnight. Cole and I are bundled in dark clothes and walk hand in hand through the trees bordering the walking path.

We still haven't talked, really talked, about all that's happened. But I know from his hand holding mine, from the smile over this morning's coffee and his palm at the small of my back as I reached to put away plates, that things are different.

Part of me, I think, should feel angry, Enraged even, that he could think such a thing of me. But I don't. Maybe that will come later. Maybe it won't. All I know is that he still loves me, and after nearly losing that, losing him, nothing else matters. And I'm not sure that if the tables were turned, I wouldn't have reacted in the exact same way. It's like imagining oneself in the throes of a life-threatening emergency. You want to believe that you'd be the one to throw yourself in front of the truck to save the old woman, or off a bridge to rescue the drowning child, but would you?

The sound of our footfalls are quiet. The leaves are muted now by the soft, new grass sprouting up under and around them. Their decay provides nutrients and nourishment to the fresh batch of summer growth—a perfect cycle of life.

We are close now, within a quarter mile of the clearing. My gut twists, the same sensation I used to get before going on stage in grade school. There are certain specifications Officer Chevalier outlined, requirements for my being allowed here tonight. No weapons (obviously), no interrupting the officers' work, no interference with the natural occurrence of events.

"No problem," I said.

Cole added, "And I am coming along. You can save yourself the fuss of arguing."

I squeeze his hand now, and then let go, letting him fall in step behind me. We move nearly soundlessly, tree frogs trilling loudly. The birds' songs begin to hush with the falling darkness. The air is brisk, and I imagine that the grass will be thick with white frost in the morning. I lead Cole to the spot where I first saw the Indian woman. We sit, knees drawn up, shoulders touching.

"This is a stake out," Chevalier had warned. "We've got no proof that they'll be coming back here tonight. This could be hours and hours of cold, boring sitting in the woods with no results. You understand that, right?" He'd looked at Cole first, then me, his gaze lingering. I nodded, and Cole gave an affirmative answer.

Our plan is to just be present. To watch. Chevalier and his sidekick are positioned on the far side of the clearing, equipped with night binoculars and other high-tech gear that I didn't realize the city had in its budget. Cole and I have been instructed that we are, "not to interact, move, make noise or get in our way," and following these guidelines we're sitting, as quiet as well-behaved mice.

The stone alter is a dark blob among a field that looks silver in the upcoming moon. The long grasses sway with a wind I can barely feel, though leaves rustle above my head. There is no other movement. I look around periodically, watching the trees not for our neighbors but for the old woman. I see no one.

The hot packs I put in my mittens and boots are working their magic. I take a deep breath of the bracing air and feel, strangely, content. It's peaceful here, just outside the clearing, and the sound of the wind sighing through the branches of the pines overhead and the smell of loam and grass lull me into a sort of sleepy trance.

I must have drifted off because I jerk awake when Cole gently shakes my shoulder. It takes a second to get my bearings, and then I look automatically out to the clearing. There is a snap of branches to the left of us, far enough away I don't worry about us being seen. Another snap, then the whine and scratch of branches sliding over nylon as a figure dressed in black appears in the clearing.

He's medium height, thin, wearing a dark knit cap. He glances in our direction. It's Bevins, and for one horrible moment I think he can see me after all. But then his eyes scan the rest of the tree line surrounding the clearing, and I let out a breath I didn't know I was holding.

The trees behind him part, and another man, the same one I saw yesterday with the gun, Marc, steps out. Charlotte trails several steps after, blond curls protruding from a fur-lined hat. For once, she's silent. Another woman follows Charlotte, then a man. On and on they stream from the woods in a single-file line walking slowly. They don't speak but gather soundlessly around the stone altar.

Bevins stands behind the altar, Marc to his left. The psychiatrist's hands rest on the stone slab, fingers ungloved and spread wide. They look out of proportion to his body, longer and thinner than fingers should look. I shiver.

Counting quickly, I note thirteen people total. The moonlight sheds enough light that I can make out faces. I see the woman who lives across the street in the large Cape Cod style house, the one I tried to talk to that morning after the ordeal with Bevins. A lot of the others don't look familiar to me. But then, they wouldn't. The conversation I had weeks ago with Cole about never seeing our neighbors floats into my head. How had he explained it away? The weather, I think. Cole presses my hand now, as though reading my thoughts.

"I'm so sorry," he whispers into my ear. "I'm so sorry I doubted you." I smile, wetness pricking my eyes, and return the squeeze with my own hand. Bevins says something, and our attention is drawn to him immediately.

"We come together tonight under the Sprouting Grass Moon, a symbol of the return of warmer days and longer nights. We thank our Earth Mother for bringing us here tonight to enjoy the bounty She's laid before us," Bevins pauses, hands lifting up toward the trees surrounding the clearing.

This doesn't sound so bad.

"And we give thanks to our Father below, the one who is always present, always steady, for the power and life-force he provides us today and always."

Uh-oh.

Bevins motions to Marc, and he extracts the metal container from beneath the stone table. It opens with a creak, and then he turns, holds the open end toward Bevins. He reaches inside, extracts something wrapped in material—the book with the pentagram on the front. The book is unwrapped, then set gently on the stone while Bevins lights each of the white candles. Marc extracts glass hurricane globes from his backpack, placing one over each candle that's struggling to stay lit with the light breeze. Inside the glass, the flames flicker and grow. Next, he takes the packet of salt, walks slowly around the outskirts of the circle of people, pouring it out like sand, forming an enclosure. Bevins opens to a certain page of the small book. The sheets of paper seem to glow in the moonlight.

He begins to speak, softly at first, nearly a whisper. Reading from the pages, words that I can't make out tumble from his lips. As he continues, the words grow louder and begin to weave themselves together in a sort of herky-jerky rhythm. His voice rises slightly, then falls, like ocean waves. His voice is melodic, restful. Though I can't understand the language spoken, a sort of lulling peace moves over me.

Marc continues around the circle of bodies, tossing the salt to the ground as Bevins speaks. The doctor stoops, pausing for breath I think, but then, no. He motions to Marc who holds up the first candle and nods to the half-circle of people in front of them. Two men step forward, one with something dark in his hand. They bend low behind the table. I hear the zipper of the bag whine open, then there is silence. No frogs, no birds, no words.

Several minutes pass in absolute silence. Then one of the men rises to his feet, nods. Bevins begins reading again. The man holds the dark object in his hands then raises it to the silver sky. The black cloth falls away, and a long, pointed silver knife is offered to the moon.

He sinks down again, behind the altar and hidden from view. I'm shivering but not cold. Rising to my haunches to get a better look, a branch pokes my side. I shift my weight, brush it aside.

Bevins is speaking again, the light from the white candles bouncing. Shimmery shadows play around the altar, around Bevins who continues reading then pauses again. He nods to Marc who holds up the second candle. There is a soft thumping coming from behind the altar. I strain my eyes but see nothing.

The people standing in front of the altar begin to murmur quietly, as Bevins intones another phrase I can't understand. They repeat the words back and forth, slow and well-worn like a Hail Mary. Their voices grow louder as the verses go on, rising and bending, gentle then louder, like the sea—waves of words.

Just as the voices rise again, sounding strong and hard in the gentle night air, there is sudden silence. Bevins raises both hands to the group, and they all end on the same note, a hush falling over the clearing. The men from behind the altar rise together holding between them the head of the pig.

{Chapter Thirty-four}

Dark blood, gummy from the cold, pools around the pig's neck as though it's wearing a thin collar. Its dead eyes stare out at the group. Bevins gestures to Marc who holds up the third candle. The two men slowly lower the head to the altar. It sits as though part of the table, the moonlight making everything silver and gray.

Bevins begins to repeat the words from earlier, in a soft singsong voice. The hair on my neck rises as his words grow louder and faster. The people in front of the altar are changing too, their voices growing loud and fast. Like a locomotive gaining speed, their fervor increases, becomes almost frantic. For full, long minutes the words continue. A man near the back begins to groan loudly. A woman in the middle of the circle raises her arms and face toward the sky, a smile stretching wide over her teeth. Then the chant turns into a scream as one of the women closest to the altar falls to the ground. She lies there, gyrating against the earth, arms outstretched, heaving up and down as though a giant, invisible hand has pulled her to the grassy floor and holds her there pinned.

Where the hell is Chevalier?

Just then Bevins speaks again, loud and clear against the backdrop of the voices crying out around him. The steadiness of it seems to quiet the others, and their voices, too, drop back to a quieter pitch. Even the woman on the ground moves more feebly.

"Brothers and sisters of the night, we come together tonight to celebrate the Sprouting Grass

Moon, just as the native ancestors who lived here long ago did. We call now upon the dead buried here, that their wisdom and souls would appear to us this night. We call upon the spirits of those asleep in this soil to rise up!"

Bevins' voice becomes loud once again, and the group moans in response then begins to beat the earth, their chests, and legs with clenched fists. They scream, "Rise up!" and "Come be with us!" intermittently.

"We offer you tonight, souls of the deep, the chance of new life. A chance to walk among us under the moon as we honor this new season of life. Come, be with us now."

The crowd is frenzied, yelling and pounding loudly in response to the deep timbre of Bevins' voice. This lasts several minutes until there is one, high, piercing scream. Charlotte falls to her knees, her head dropping forward over her chest and stomach until it touches the earth. She's moaning quietly. Then the sound gets louder.

"Where the hell is that cop?" Cole whispers loudly near my ear. I'm transfixed by what's happening in front of me.

"Stand, daughter of the night," Bevins commands.

Charlotte is silent for a full minute then jerks to her feet, her arms and legs disjointed like a marionette. She stands, swaying in front of the altar.

"Daughter, we are glad you've come," says Bevins. Charlotte doesn't move or acknowledge his voice. There is silence for several long minutes. Then murmuring begins among the crowd.

"Hisho," they murmur collectively. "Hisho." They string the word together, so that the end of one flows into the beginning of another. *HishoHishoHishoHishoHisho.*

Finally, Charlotte's body jerks. Her hands grip the edge of the altar, and she uses it to turn herself to face the crowd.

I look at her face and gasp then palm my mouth to muffle the sound. Her expression is twisted, eyes slits, mouth wide and pulled back over her teeth.

A voice that doesn't sound like a woman's comes from her body.

"We are with you, brothers and sisters."

Charlotte twitches, then turns back to the altar and grasps the head of the dead pig in both of her small hands. She heaves it up above her head and in one deft motion throws it far into the clearing. It bounces twice before rolling to a stop. The group stands motionless, watching, then turn with anxious faces toward her. She grimaces again, her features seeming to slide to one side of her face before coming back to the snarl.

"This does not please us . . . this imposter," her voice raises into a growl, spit flying from her taut mouth as she points an accusing finger toward the head in the field.

"You think so little of us that this is the sacrifice you offer? A dead swine. A dead swine?" The last words come out as a screech, and for a moment I think she's going to levitate into the air, flatten the crowd. The men and women cower in front of her, shaking their heads. Bevins' head is bowed, his long fingers spread once again on the stone table. She jerks her head back to him, snarling like a wolf and grabs his hands. The force with which she yanks him forward is so hard and fast that his rib bones crack against the table. He cries out, and I feel Cole tense behind me. I place a hand on his arm, shake my head.

"Where the hell is the damn cop?" He asks again. I shake my head again, turn back to watch the drama around the altar. My pulse is fluttering fast in my palms, and sweat has broken out across my forehead and down my spine.

"We are sorry, dark sister," Bevins says, his voice a high whine. He coughs once, twice. Charlotte seems to loosen her grip as an inch of space appears between the man's ribcage and the altar.

They stand motionless for one minute. Two. The crowd is unmoving making the whole scene look like a photo. Surreal. Then Chevalier and the other officer sprint from the tree line opposite Cole and I. They are low to the ground, moving fast.

Another screech erupts from Charlotte, and she lets go of Bevins' hands, crumples to the ground in a heap. Bevins lays across the stone table, unmoving. The others run, a jagged line of men and women but then split into many different directions, like ants whose hill has just been decimated.

Chevalier moves to where Bevins lies across the altar, checks his pulse, seems satisfied when the man groans in response. He moves behind him, propping him up. Charlotte is on the ground and still doesn't move. Her curls are tangled and her thin frame pulled into a fetal position. I want to go to her, start to move in that direction but Cole holds me back.

"You promised, Sarah."

"That was before I knew they were going to possess Charlotte," I hiss. But then I sink back into Cole's chest, let him smooth my hair away from my face. "I know," I say. "I remember." Then, "Do you think she's OK?"

Cole is watching the second officer bending over Charlotte, checking her breathing. We both sigh in unison when we hear him tell Chevalier that she's breathing but unconscious.

An hour later, Cole and I are back in the great room watching the whirling lights of the ambulance retreat down the central drive. Bevins is onboard. Charlotte was taken earlier, an oxygen mask strapped over her white, waxy face.

A knock at the door makes me jump. Answering the door, Cole invites the person inside. Chevalier stands in the foyer. He looks even smaller under the high ceilings and chandelier, like a little boy playing policeman. His face doesn't look childish though, just tired and gray.

"Can I get you something to drink?" Cole asks. I stand dumbly near the window trying to rouse myself from this stupor.

"Coffee would be great." Chevalier follows Cole into the kitchen, and I trail behind on wooden legs.

"What happens now?" Cole asks as the three of us lean against the granite bar. There are two tables in the room, but it feels like too much effort to rearrange ourselves at one of them.

Chevalier takes a sip of coffee, nods his thanks.

"Dunno. He'll be out soon, Dr. Bevins. I'm sure of it. He told me his attorney is Paul Andress. You've heard of him?"

Cole and I shake our heads.

"He's the best attorney in the state. Went head-to-head with the former governor himself over a hunting permit issue. Won, of course. He wins them all." Chevalier's voice drifts off as he stares into his cup.

"So he'll be back here at Hawthorne Estates?" I ask. My voice sounds creaky. "When? A week? A month?"

"Two days, maybe. By the end of the week the latest I'd guess."

Two days.

{Chapter Thirty-five}

My head suddenly feels too heavy for my shoulders. My neck aches. I prop my elbows on the counter, face buried within. They smell like dryness and lilac soap.

"So what's the next step?" Cole asks. I listen, eyes closed. My breath is loud in my ears.

Chevalier is silent for a moment then responds.

"He shouldn't have contact with you. In fact, you'll likely want a restraining order, make it official. What happened in the woods. . ." his voice drifts away momentarily. "Well, there wasn't an actual crime. Bevins stated that the pig was dead, found it near the road and used it for their," Chevalier sips his coffee, "ceremony."

I snort, raising my face to look at him.

"Found it on the side of the road. Like that chipmunk he was gnawing on?"

Chevalier shakes his head slightly.

"Problem with the law is that we don't have any evidence. We need cold, hard facts in order to prove anything. And having a satanic ritual, while disturbing, isn't illegal. Freedom of religion and all that. We'd need evidence. Either that they maimed an animal or hurt a person. If everyone is there of their own free will, well. . . "

"You'd need hard facts in order to build a case against him, you mean." Cole's voice is quiet, reflective. I look at him. He's looking past Chevalier and me to the far bank of windows, black now, mirroring our images back.

"I wouldn't go so far as to even call this a case," Chevalier raises his hand at my protest. "Not yet. You've got to get the culprit telling you things on a wire, abducting a person or trying to harm someone. A person," Chevalier takes another gulp of coffee, "not a chipmunk, and you'll have the beginning of a case."

"So, we need to wait until he hurts a human, is that it?" My voice is louder than I intended. The cup in my hand rattles as I set it abruptly down in its saucer. "Why don't I just offer myself up to them? Sacrificial lamb and all that?" Hardness has woven itself through my throat, and I set my tongue between my teeth to avoid saying more.

"I'm sorry," I say after several minutes of uncomfortable silence. "I just don't agree with the legal system here."

Cole nods. "But we're not going to be rash, officer. We promise."

Both men look at me. I swallow the hard ball in my throat and force a smile.

"Of course not," I say.

But I don't mean it. If being rash will get something done, then I'll be as bloody well rash as possible.

Cole shows Chevalier out moments later. I retreat to my art room, wander around touching paint tubes and pads of thick drawing paper. I end up before the only wall that has any artwork on it. I've broken my own rule of not hanging my own work in the studio. Perched on the wall with pushpins are the sketches of the old Abenaki woman from the forest. Cole comes up behind me, arms around my waist. He rests his chin on the top of my head.

"Who is she, do you think?" he asks.

I stare at the sketch, willing it to give me an answer. The gray woman stares back, at some point far beyond me. Her eyes are filled with an emotion I can't quite place. Angst? No, something sad, more painful. The look is one I know but can't put my finger on.

"I'm not sure."

I move out of Cole's embrace, squeeze his arm as he turns to leave the room.

"I'm going to take a shower," he calls over his shoulder. I nod absently.

Moving closer to the sketch, I block out the rest of the room, the wall and the paper, until I'm staring only into the woman's gray eyes. But they aren't looking at me.

"What do you see?" I whisper. I stare into her eyes, willing the paper to talk to me. And suddenly I recognize the emotion I see there. *Longing.* My breath catches in my throat. I remember where the woman stood, on the edge of the clearing, the eastern side. I take the sketch from the wall not bothering to unpin it first. The tack cuts a small, jagged line through the edge of the paper.

I move soundlessly, place the sketch against the wall farthest from me, stab another tack through the top. This is the same direction she was standing when I saw her. I leave the paper there, move to the opposite end of the room pretending my studio is the clearing. I was positioned here, facing this direction, the first time I saw her. I look to the sketch now. My heart stumbles over itself.

She is looking past me, away into what would be the far side of the clearing. Longing fills her otherwise impassive face. What was it? What did she see?

The next morning, I'm awake and dressed before the first pink wash has covered the eastern sky. The air is chilly. Standing on the front stoop I gather the mail from yesterday. The neighbor's house is shuttered and dark, but a shiny black Jaguar sits in the driveway.

Leaving the mail on the hall table, I grab a small bag and go out again, pulling the door closed behind me. The smell is intoxicating: fresh pine, cold earth, the leftover scent of stars. The bag holds a sketch book and pencil, one nubby eraser. I don't know what I'm looking for or what I might find, but it doesn't hurt to be prepared. I follow the walking path behind the house as it curls through the forest, flattens out near the small brook. I stop for a minute, listen to the swell of the frogs' voices in the early morning air, watch the water bouncing and burbling over a mosaic of stones. Then I turn, continue on.

The path nearest the clearing is dense, the forest leaves thick. Despite the frosty air, leaves are halfway open. They rustle softly as I step off the path following the bent grass into the clearing.

The sound of the leaves is still here, the air heavy and silent. I ignore the hair standing up on my arms and skirt the stone altar looking for the place where I stood when I came here for the first time. The altar looks smaller in daylight, and though I've told myself not to look, my eyes are drawn there as to the scene of an accident. A dark red ring of blood is dried onto the stone where the pig's head had been placed. Smears of it run along the stone, and I shiver when I see the decapitated body lying stiff behind the altar. Something has been eating at it already; I see flesh torn away near the hind end.

I look away. *Focus.* Nearly every side of the clearing looks the same to me, but I remember approximately where I stepped out of the tree line that first day. I walk to the spot, pause. Look to the far right where the woman stood. *There?* No, too many tree branches. And then I realize that it will look different now because of the undergrowth and the trees which have leafed out. I scan the clearing, try to pinpoint the spot. Branches tentatively test the air, poking just into the clearing enough to make it difficult for me to remember.

There. That spot. I remember the tree nearest the woman was tall, one of the tallest here, old and craggy. Its bark looks ready to collapse off the trunk, in tough, brown chunks. Closing my eyes, I blank out thoughts. It's an old trick, one I use frequently as an artist. When the image in my mind isn't coming through on the canvas or when my brain is too busy sorting things out and making lists, I do this. Breathe in, study the blackness, form a blank slate behind my eyelids then breathe out.

I'm quiet for several minutes, but when I open my eyes, I see her again, as though on that first day. She's standing straight and tall, the old, craggy tree to her left and slightly behind. She's beautiful, strong, the thick braid draped over her shoulder pulled through with gray. Her face looks at that far away spot on the opposite end of the clearing, eyes full of longing. Then a shadow passes over, and in a second her eyes are turned toward me, watching, like a deer that's just spotted a hunter.

She is motionless, and then, just like the first day, I glance away and remember that when I turn back she'll be gone. This time I don't speak or move in the direction where she once stood, though. Instead I follow her line of sight, looking to the opposite end of the clearing. I see nothing but trees.

The walk across the clearing is longer than I thought it would be. The tall grass that waved silver in the moonlight last night pulls on my ankles. Only early spring, I imagine that by mid-summer it will be waist high. The ground underneath is uneven, several times I stub my toe on large, smooth stones. It's like walking into lake water when you can't see the bottom. I move more slowly, feeling my way with my feet though they're hidden beneath the green waves of the field grass.

Finally, I am on the other side. It looks nearly identical to the opposite tree line, and for a moment, I'm disheartened. Looking back, I see the jagged line through the grass I've made. Then I turn to the trees in front of me, the branches here moving gently.

I look up into the branches then down around the low lying bushes but see nothing. I think about the woman's face, Josie Little Fish. Her eyes, filled with such angst. Why? What did she see here? Or was it just a memory she had of this place?

I get down into a crouch, search the ground in and around the trees. Branches and tall grass are woven among dead leaves in various states of decomposition. Stones in different sizes and berry bushes, their pointed thorns already emerging sharp from the waxy branches. There must be something.

Widening my search area, a memory comes to me. An outdoor adventure challenge from college, a sort of treasure hunt. The seekers were equipped with coordinates and a hand held GPS unit. Hidden somewhere in the vicinity was a cache, sometimes small enough to hold only a scrap of paper which you could add your name to, sometimes as large as a shoe box filled with trinkets and a log book.

Twenty-five minutes later I'm beginning to sweat. My hands are covered in dirt which has worked its way up under my nails. Grass stains cover the knees of my jeans, and my hair has bits of bark and tiny tree branches in it.

I finally give up and sit, pressing my back against the smooth trunk of a poplar. A bird chirps loudly overhead, and far away I hear the drone of an airplane. Disappointment burns the back of my throat. Maybe Josie was simply remembering how this place used to be. Remembering something that happened here years ago. Maybe she was daydreaming for all I know.

But those eyes . . . that expression. I push a frizzy curl out of my face, turn to stretch my neck. And then I see it. Twenty feet from where I'm sitting and half-covered in a wash of dry brown leaves—a small stone.

A headstone.

{Chapter Thirty-six}

I scramble across the distance, half running, half crawling. My hands are sweeping away the leaves before I've even had a chance to wonder how this got here, who is buried here beneath this stone.

I'm disappointed by my find. The rock's surface is smooth and light brown, more rounded than square, and there is no name on it. But as I bend closer, fingers lightly skimming the surface, I feel the engraving. Not a name in English, but words and letters placed in an order that I don't recognize. A different language. The rain and snow has eroded the surface, so that it's hard to tell where smoothness ends and lettering begins. I close my eyes and move my fingertips lightly over the cold rock feeling my way over it as though it's Braille. For one crazy moment, I wonder if I can lift the stone, take it with me. Then I remember my bag.

Pulling it close to me, I rifle through and extract the pencil, tearing a sheet of the thin sketch paper. Fingers chilly, I press the pencil horizontally against the paper, rubbing in slow, even patches. It reminds me of grade school, when the entire class was released into a graveyard with paper and crayons to make rubbings of the ancient grave markers. Slowly, tediously, the characters begin to emerge. The work is meditative, the birds overhead tweeting and chirping, a cool breeze teasing curls around my face.

A branch breaks startling me to the present. I glance to my right but see only trees and shrubbery, the same thing on the left. No movement, nothing out of the ordinary. I stretch my neck then resume the rubbing. Near the bottom I stop, squint then bend close. Where the characters above are soft and partially eroded by the elements, here, close to the bottom, they are more distinct. My breath catches as I recognize these characters emerging on the paper. It feels like a secret code, like I'm ten years old again living a Nancy Drew mystery. Two numbers, followed by two more and then four. The last are so badly eroded I can't make them out, but I know what this is. A date. April 15th.

I sit back on my heels, mind whirling. That date is familiar to me, but why? And then it hits me. It's the date from the newspaper, the date of the initial dig when the contractor, Smith, had the state officials on this land. The one that the three Abenaki council members had protested.

Why engrave that date on this stone? The brown lump of rock sits silently amid the pile of leaves. I sink back onto the forest floor, paper in hand, soft moss and scratchy twigs poking my rear end. What was it that the article had said? There had been an investigation by the state officials. No evidence of human remains found. But there was something else, something niggling at the back of my mind like a persistent mosquito.

Another branch snaps, this time I'm pretty sure it's across the clearing. Eyes scan that way; I shiver again at the outline of the altar and the dark stain. Nothing. No movement. Goose bumps rise on my arms, though, and the hair at the base of my neck stands on end. I gather the paper, place it carefully back into the hard sketchbook, tuck the pencil back into its case, all the while keeping one eye on the trees waiting for someone in black to jump out and grab me.

Despite the fear, I feel victorious. I've gotten what I came for: an answer to the expression in Josie Little Fish's eyes. I'll bring the paper to John but am relatively sure I know what the letters on the gravestone spell—the old Abenaki woman's daughter's name.

"So you found it," the voice cuts through the morning air like a knife, deep and close by. I gasp, whirl around. A figure stands behind me dressed in jeans and a dark blue windbreaker, a ball cap pulled down low over his eyes. Tall, with lean muscles. A perfect flash of white when he grins. Cy St. Francis.

"Figured it was just a matter of time. You're what The People would call . . . hmmm, I forget my Abenaki tongue sometimes. But in regular old English, you're what we'd call nosy. Didn't get the message at the library, did you, Sarah?"

My voice sounds rusty in my throat. "That was you?"

"Nah," Cy gives a shake of his head, slow, nearly bored looking. "Not me. But I knew it was in the works." He looks away from me for a minute, across the clearing toward the altar. "Looks like Bevins has been at it again."

"If by 'at it' you mean making animal sacrifices in some sort of demon-possessed ritual, then yes, he has." I'm amazed at my ability to form words. My heart chatters away in my chest.

"Just how much of this," I pause, wave a hand toward the clearing, "do you know about?"

The smile comes out again, a quick flash. I notice that Cy has a dimple on the left cheek. His dark hair is pulled back into a ponytail behind the cap, making his high brown cheekbones more prominent.

"Most of it, I have to admit Mrs. Solomon. Oh that's right, you said I could call you Sarah, didn't you?" He goes on without pausing. "I've been working with Dr. Bevins for many years. Since Smith built this place in fact," he nods in the direction of the community of houses.

"It's a special place," he says.

Oh yeah, it's special all right.

He's silent for a moment, looking out past the forest. My brain is moving at warp speed, facts and information coming in bits and pieces and matching up so quickly I can barely keep it all straight. I want to suddenly smack my forehead in disbelief at my obvious oversight. *Smith. Developer. Cy. Realtor. Our home. Knife.*

"It's you," I breathe out, not even conscious that I've put all the pieces together, yet here they are. I can't believe I missed it.

"It's been you all this time. Breaking into our home, setting things up. The artwork . . . the knife. The photocopies and the note in the holly . . . you had access. You have, what, a key? No sign of a break in, that's what Officer Chevalier said. Of course, there's no sign. Why would there be?"

Cy smiles again, this time it's slow, savoring the moment. "Very good, Sarah. Perhaps if you hadn't been an artist you could have gone into work as a private investigator. Yes, I have a key," he says it matter of fact as though I asked the time of day. "Have had since before you moved in. One of the perks of being a realtor, and there are precious few these days. Market's in the toilet, but we're all still out there smiling our winning smiles and talking about the great opportunities and stellar chances that buyers have." He shakes his head.

"Bevins hired me," he offers, "to take care of your house. He got the photocopies of your time in the looney bin, though. Easy enough. Simple phone call to a colleague in Philadelphia. Unfortunately, you're a little more hard-headed than we anticipated." He smiles at me wryly like he's chastising a kid who forgot to wipe his muddy shoes. "It's not you, Sarah, I hope you understand that. At least, it wasn't anything personal before you started sticking your nose where it doesn't belong."

"Not personal?" My voice cracks, and I have the crazy desire to laugh. "Oh, well, that makes me feel very good. Thanks for that."

"You shouldn't have bought that house, Sarah. Hawthorne Estates is," Cy breaks off momentarily, "exclusive. It wasn't meant for just anyone to live here. But when your husband swooped in and made the purchase, used another realtor in town and paid more than the asking price, well, it was completely out of the blue. Unexpected. We had another buyer all picked out, you know. After the debacle with the Rainville family we knew that the buyers had to be selected with care. And you and your husband, my dear, were not what we were looking for."

"We? Are you part of this little group?" I nod my head in the direction of the clearing, the stone altar.

Cy laughs easily.

"Oh no, nothing like that. What Bevins and his crew does here is entirely his business. I'm just the," he breaks off for a moment, "connector, I guess is a good word. I look for the best possible match for whatever it is my client needs and see that they get it. No matter what."

"And what was it that your client wanted here?"

"Well, privacy of course. But you already know what else they looked for, don't you? Why this spot was chosen?"

I think back to the newspaper articles, the council members and the words Bevins himself said last night. A hand goes automatically to my throat, an old habit. I stare into Cy's handsome face.

"It's true then? This is a, a. . ." my voice breaks off then starts again. "A burial ground?"

Cy nods, smiles again.

"That's what my clients asked for, and that's what they got."

"But the State did tests. I read about it. Surely Smith wasn't able to bribe all the officials involved in covering this up?"

Cy chuckles, rocks back on his heels slightly. "There wasn't anything to cover up. Not at that point."

I rack my brain, trying to understand. The mosquito thought flits in again but then back out. I am silent for a full minute, then two. Trying desperately to catch the thought, pin it down. And then it comes to me.

"The storm. The ground that was disturbed—I read about it in the article. It wasn't a storm, was it? That was . . . you're a grave robber." The end of my sentence fades out, barely audible, as though I just moved away from a mic.

"Let's not get dramatic, Sarah. First of all, I have never disturbed the resting place of my kin. Or anyone, for that matter. All of those types of details were left to those in charge—Smith and Bevins. They knew the location, knew what it held and that was part of the draw for them.

"Secondly, no one knew about this parcel here," Cy nods toward the clearing behind us. "None of the state officials, I mean. This land isn't even part of the plot that Smith bought. This tract is owned by the state now, never to be developed. Too bad," Cy looks around the forest with longing. "Some old farmer left it as protected property in a land trust.

"The burial ground the council was disputing was right where Hawthorne Estates is now. Just a few bodies—four, maybe five. Those were, unfortunately, right where Smith had plans to build. But it worked out well since Bevins was looking for a property with, well, shall I say previous tenants?" Cy laughs, white teeth flash.

"So we moved them. Simple as that. What do they care? They're dead. Anyway, I told you I'm just the connector. I bring the pieces together. Smith and Bevins worked out the specifics."

"I hope you don't think that makes you any less guilty," I spit the words out, anger heating my gut, burning my cheeks red. "You're just as bad as they are. Worse, maybe. You sold your own people to them! You desecrated graves. For what? Money? Power? How can you live with . . ." A sharp crack across the face shocks me. Pain follows close on the heels of the surprise. I stumble, fall to one knee. Cy's hand falls back to his side.

"Shut up." Cy's words are even, mild, as though he asked me to pass the salt.

"You don't know what you're talking about. You don't know the first thing about growing up Indian, growing up different. Don't talk to me about 'your people.' What do you know about me, Sarah? Nothing. Do you know what being Abenaki has gotten me? Grief. Heartache. Beaten up when I was a kid and passed by for jobs as an adult. I carry the damn stigma around with me like a brand, a tattoo. Well, I never asked for it. I never asked to be part of the clan. The clan can fuck themselves. It's every man for himself now; we're not defending the homeland against the encroaching English. The English are here! You should know—you're one of them. Now I am, too."

Hand to my face, I press my cool palm into the hotness of my cheek. My heartbeat thunders loud in my ears threatening to drown out Cy's ranting.

"But the people buried here, what happened to them?" My voice sounds more normal in my ears than I could have imagined possible. I twist sideways, still propped on one knee and look at the man before me.

Cy chuckles again, left hand in his jacket pocket. The knuckles of his right hand are red, and my cheek throbs harder.

"Well, Sarah, the great thing about excavating for a new, multimillion dollar project like this is all the opportunities it creates. Most people don't know a lot about the Abenaki form of burial. No headstones were used, and the graves tended to be shallow. The dead were wrapped in birch bark, no coffin, and buried with their greatest earthly treasures.

"The gravesites were usually near a village. Here, there were only a few bodies actually found during excavation; the rest likely reside in the clearing." Cy points to the open space where the grass undulates in a breeze. "The ones we found at the site were disposed of."

"Where?"

Cy smiles, shakes his head as though I'm a naughty school girl or a toddler with too many questions.

"Sarah, have you spent any time near the pond?"

"The pond. . ." I think about the beautiful, happy sounds of gurgling water, the streams feeding the pond tucked into the grove of trees near my house. The frogs trilling in the night air, the water, peaceful and calm.

"You put bodies in there?"

Cy shakes his head.

"Not bodies. Just bones and the old junk that we found with them—arrows and quivers and in one case, an antique gun. Too rusted to use or even try to sell. The women weren't buried with as much, baskets, some junk we couldn't identify."

My head is whirling, my thoughts tumbling over and around each other disjointed and fragmented.

"And this one?" I ask, pointing to the small, round stone. "This one does have a headstone. Who is it?"

Cy looks at the stone then taps it with the toe of his hiking boot. I want to kick him.

"Josie Little Fish's daughter, Elaina Rose. Kid died when she was a toddler. Accident of some kind. Josie was likely drunk or spending the night with someone who was. Rumors say that my father beat the bitch up, that he was to blame for Elaina's death. But that's a bunch of rubbish. My old man was a womanizer, no doubt. But I never saw him hit a woman. Josie was probably drunk or stoned, would have been hauled in on child abuse charges, negligence, endangerment, all sorts of ugly stuff. So she ran away and killed herself. Or just ran off. Maybe she's living in New York City now, or maybe she drowned herself or fell off a cliff. Who knows?" Cy says, a smirk marring his beautiful face. "Maybe she's still creeping around in the woods, living off berries and trapped animals like our ancestors. Like an animal."

"You're despicable."

A laugh rumbles from his chest. "Better despicable than defenseless. And that, my dear Sarah, is exactly what you are. Defenseless and stupid. Did you really think nosing around in other people's lives would bring you anything but pain?"

"But why is the stone here?" I ask, stalling for time. "Why date it the same day as the start of excavation at Hawthorne Estates?"

Cy is shaking his head again, slow and even. Then he sighs.

"Enough questions, Sarah. That's what got you into this mess, isn't it?" He pulls his left hand from his pocket. In it is a gun. Snub-nosed. Black.

I watch in horror, limbs suddenly iced-over, as he points it directly at my face.

{Chapter Thirty-seven}

"Walk," he says, and motions toward the deeper forest behind us. I look frantically toward the clearing, but it's empty, silent. The birds overhead have quieted, and for one breathless moment time seems to stop. The world around me grows gray, a familiar tunnel appearing just outside my peripheral vision. My breath is ragged, choking. I start to shake, and my heartbeat speeds up even faster, though I didn't think it possible. I recognize the signs. Panic skitters beneath my skin. *Not now. Not now.*

"Move," Cy says, and the smile has left his face. His eyes narrow, but I can barely see him as the world around me grows darker. And then I'm moving backward in time, to that night . . . I've tried so hard to forget it.

The blackness of the sky, no moon or stars. My hands pressing tight on the wheel, a slight swerve, then the blue lights flashing. The officer standing beside my car, then grabbing, hands hard and strong like steel bands on my arms. My scream when I realized what was happening, then the strike of his gun against my head. Cotton ball brain, moving through molasses. I stopped struggling and focused on simply breathing, making myself float out of my body when hands tore at my skirt, cold belt buckle pressed against my back. Pain. I looked up toward the cloudless sky, and wished I were part of it; far away. Anywhere but there.

"Don't pass out on me, Sarah," Cy's voice jolts me back to the present. The gun still aims between my eyes. Slowly the gray around my vision begins to lift, like fog dissipating. I take deep, slow breaths.

"That's a good girl," he says, then waves the gun toward the woods again. I walk. My feet feel weighted with rocks, my legs shaky with adrenaline that has nowhere to go. I stretch my hands out in front of me, warding off whip-like branches and pine needles. Some make it through my barricade, though, leaving welts against my cheeks and pine pitch on my neck and in my hair.

We walk for ten minutes, then fifteen. Where are we going? What will he do with my body once I'm . . . But I stop myself. I'm not dead yet. I can still get out of this, get away. I need to think, use my brain. Everything feels slow and syrupy though. I look to the right, then the left, but all of it looks the same. Trees and outcroppings of rock, dead leaves and new baby grass. I think of Cole. I wish we'd properly made up. My breath starts coming fast again, and I will myself not to give in, not to cry. There must be something I can do . . .

"Stop here," Cy says. I stop, rest my hand against the bark of a birch tree. Cy moves in front of me, gun still raised.

"I'm sorry it had to come to this, Sarah. You can't say you weren't warned. You chose not to listen," Cy looks genuinely sorrowful, and for one brief moment I think maybe I can talk my way out of this.

"You don't have to do this, Cy. You can still change things. Let me go. I'll leave the neighborhood quietly. I swear it."

Cy's sad look changes instantly to a smile, and I realize that the sorrow was just a show.

"I'm sorry, but that's not an option."

I stare at him mutely. For one instant all the fog in my mind clears, and I see a possible solution, a potential chance. I grasp it like a rope dangling over a cliff. Cy is looking at me, his face darkened by what? Anger, distaste. I wonder how he was the one to get stuck with this job. Or perhaps he volunteered. If the money was right, I'm sure there wasn't much hesitation. And what I do next cannot involve hesitation either. Before my thinking clouds, before the fear blocks out reality again, I have to move. I have to try. I stand, facing Cy, hands loose by my sides.

I've only got one shot.

"So, are you going to shoot me while you look me in the eyes?" I ask. "I bet you're too much of a coward. Going to make me turn around, maybe kneel down execution-style?"

Cy motions with his hand, another smile spreading over his handsome face. This one is half grimace, though, and twists his mouth.

"Despite what you think, Sarah, I'm not looking forward to this."

"Then don't do it. Leave me here. I won't tell a soul, I won't . . ." Then I gasp, my hands outstretched, looking past Cy into the forest beyond. "Oh, thank God!" I say into the empty air.

Cy pauses, momentarily confused. He looks quickly behind him, pivoting on one heel. I hunch low and plow as fast and hard as I can, adrenaline adding strength to my legs and a hardness to my

254

body. In another instant, I'm ramming all my weight into Cy's gut.

He stumbles backward. *Ooomph.* The air whooshes out of his belly. He crashes into a big oak tree. My neck reverberates with the snap as he hits it full force. I'm stunned momentarily, then turning and grappling for the gun which has slipped from his hand.

He's on me in an instant, wrestling, our sweaty fingers greasy on the barrel. I try to bite his fingers, but his elbow connects with my nose. Blood comes out, but I barely feel the pain. I get one good elbow jab into his ribcage and then try to knee him in the groin. But then his own knees are on my chest, and I can't breathe. His weight threatens to break my ribs. My fingers are loosening their hold on the gun, but I fight to keep it, to hold on. If he gets it, this is over, I'm dead. Slippery fingertips, grasping, holding, and then the gun is gone, out of my hands.

I can't breathe. Stars explode in front of my open eyes, and I wait for the blast of the bullet to rip into my forehead. I keep my eyes open, drinking in the sight of the tiny budding leaves swaying overhead, the sky blue as a robin's egg.

There is silence for a moment except for the whoosh of blood in my ears. My body is rigid, terror tightening every muscle and fiber.

Cy has rolled off me, and I can breathe, and it feels so good. Tears are running down my face. *Cole. Oh, Cole.*

Then Cy is kneeling near my head rubbing the spot in his ribs. I hope I broke one. I gasp out a half-sob, and he turns, looks at me. His ball cap has fallen off, and his ponytail has come loose. Dark hair frames his face. He gives me a twisted smile, raises the gun.

There is a crash unlike anything I've ever heard before. At first, I think the gun has gone off, but there is no pain, no blood. Then I see Cy crumple forward, blood flowing from his scalp over his face. I watch in horror as he kneels suspended before finally collapsing backward onto his heels, knees and legs pressed into the earth. Like a yogi, he stares upward at the sky, meditating on something I can't see. I sit up slowly, hands pressing against leaves and dirt. My arms tremble and shake, my body aching with fatigue.

The old Abenaki woman stands behind the crumpled body, in her hands a thick, gnarled tree branch. There is a red blossom of blood on the bark, and she is staring at it as though surprised. She looks at me then, lowering the branch to her side.

Cy's throat makes a strange wheeze. My head turns in slow motion and looks at him. He is trapped in an awkward pose, back and head pressed down to the ground, knees and legs in a prayer position beneath him. His left leg jerks twice, and then his chest stops moving.

I look back to the woman. She looks very much like the first time I saw her in the woods. Arrow straight hair in a thick gray braid, eyes hooded. But close up I see that her eyes are blue-gray, that her cheeks are sunken where teeth used to be, and that her build is more muscular than I thought. She doesn't move, just stares at Cy.

Finally, I break the silence.

"Thank you," I say, voice trembling. "You saved my life."

She looks away for a moment, back toward the woods where I walked moments ago. Again, she glances at me. There's an expression in her eyes that I can't decipher. She gives a nod so slight that I almost miss it.

I turn toward Cy. He's still motionless, staring unseeing at the peekaboo blue sky above the towering pine trees.

When I look back, she's gone.

{Epilogue}

"And so how long did you stay at your home at Hawthorne Estates after all this happened?" Erik Neil, of Vermont's popular, "Neil Show," asks. His eyes are blue, bright like a spring sky, and dark curls fall over his forehead. Lights from the filming studio make him glow, and I wonder momentarily if they are covering the sickly yellowish hue my own skin has taken on in recent months. His face is fixed in an expression of great compassion. Whether real or fake, I'm not sure. I glance down at my hands, find that they are pressed tight together. *Breathe, Sarah.*

"My husband and I left within a month after the. . ." my voice drifts uncertainly, "incident. We relocated to . . . a town in the southern part of the state shortly after that."

"Was that a hard change for you? Moving stress on top of everything else you were dealing with?"

I laugh, but it sounds hollow.

"In light of all that went on leading up to that event, the move was completely pain-free."

Erik nods, smiles, his perfect white teeth peeking out for a minute. Then his face becomes more serious.

"What can you tell me about the aftermath of this event? We all saw the court proceedings. First, the conviction of Dr. Andrew Bevins and then the estate developer, James E. Smith. But what was your reaction personally? How did it feel to hear that verdict handed down?"

I think back to that day, and as usual my memories come in fragments, photographs of my senses: the dry, musty smell of the courtroom, the tight grip of my hands on the arms of the hard wood chair, my attorney nodding to me in encouragement as I took the witness stand, the creak of the floorboards as we all listened in silence to hear the verdict read aloud. I remember that I wore a blue blouse and that my pants were wrinkled and that both ended up with teardrops wetting them. I remember doubling over, hands covering my face as Cole rubbed my back after the sentence was given. He whispered in my ear, "It's over, Sarah. It's all over. You were great."

I remember the face of Andrew Bevins as he was led from the courthouse in handcuffs. He looked at me only once, for one breathless second. I saw something in his eyes that I recognized, an emotion that I spent so long learning to overcome. Fear.

In the end, Dr. Bevins' lost his medical license and all credentials and was sentenced to six years in a federal penitentiary in Newport. He would likely be out sooner, my attorney warned. The willful disturbance of graves is a federal offense as is the conspiracy to commit murder but my attorney had little hope that Bevins would serve the full sentence.

James E. Smith fared better. The old man had dementia, and his sentence was reduced to house arrest. I watched as he tottered out of the witness's chair, the bailiff holding his elbow. Smith's hair was white, his face dotted with age spots. His eyes were fuzzy, unfocused. But he had his pride. He tried to answer the questions posed by my attorney, and then his own, but most of his responses were meandering, nonsensical.

The pond on the Estates had been emptied after an initial drag had resulted in human remains. In total, remains of five bodies were found in the muck and sludge under the water: three men and two women. Digging had begun in other areas of the Estates. The developed acreage where our homes were yielded more bones and Abenaki artifacts. Smith and Bevins denied knowing that the graves were there, but with my account and Charlotte's, the case against the developer was strengthened.

Shallow graves on the outskirts of the clearing were found. The State chose not to dig further in case more graves were desecrated. Because the land was protected by a land trust, there was no fear that further development would take place. The St. Francis tribe of Swanton were allowed to decide whether to move the remains to a new burial ground. They chose to let the dead rest where they were.

Homeowners at Hawthorne Estates were given two choices by the State: have the houses moved or have them burned to the ground. The local volunteer fire department, I heard, practiced controlled burns with seven of the nine houses, ours included. Two neighbors chose to relocate the structures to other locations.

An official, binding document between the Abenaki people and the State of Vermont was signed; a thin slip of paper with the governor's seal was turned over to the acting chief. An apology of sorts and a promise that the land protected in the trust would never be disturbed.

News crews had become a regular part of the landscape in the month or so following the initial investigation at Hawthorne Estates. The news teams waited outside the gates, explosions of flash and a barrage of questions pelting anyone going in or out of the neighborhood.

It all seemed too long ago somehow, and yet. . .

"Sarah? Can you tell me what your reaction was personally to the news of the verdict?"

Erik's voice draws me back to the present.

I clear my throat. His face is open, waiting.

"Relief of course. It was amazing after all the months of trial to see justice carried out. And I suppose in some small way, I felt a certain pleasure that I helped to make things right.

"A long time ago something really bad happened to me. I was a victim of a crime, and since that time I felt like a victim in every area of my life. But this process, as strange as it might sound, really helped me to heal. To grow. So I suppose in addition to feeling relieved, I feel very grateful."

Erik poses more questions, the lights on my face growing hot, until finally he's done, and the music that signals the end of the talk show sounds. I stand, relieved to be finished. He walks me to the door of the waiting area, thanks me for my time.

And then I'm out in the blinding sun. The leaves above are sparse, most of the brilliant burnt orange and apple red and yellow are underfoot now. They sound like whispers as I walk through City

Park. Beyond the browning grass, the sounds of Church Street meander. The smell of food wafts in this direction. Behind me lies Lake Champlain; even here in the heart of the city I'd swear I can smell the difference, feel the coolness in the breeze.

It will be a two-hour drive to our home on the outskirts of Brattleboro. Not a gated community this time, but one with real neighbors who say hello and wave when we drive past.

We chose Brattleboro because it has a great art scene: pretty little museums and funky art shops and cool cafes and stores that Cole and I have already spent a bit of time poking around in. I haven't said anything yet, but I've been imagining opening my own retail space again. Will it happen? I don't know. I still have some healing to do, but the fact that it's even a possibility is exciting. But first I need a rest. A long one.

I smile at a mother pushing a stroller, and she grins back, a two-year old pulling at her pant leg and saying, "Giddyup, Mama!" I turn left on the path, following it around and back to Church Street. I pass a beautiful wine shop on the left and pause for a moment outside the door.

"Excuse me," a man says, exiting the shop. He holds the door open for me, and I smile, shake my head *no thank you* and keep walking. I read somewhere recently that a lot more artists would do a lot less drinking if they immersed themselves in their work instead of a bottle. I'm not sure that's an accurate assessment but plan to find out. There's a colorful art supply store here that I want to visit again and a book shop just around the corner that caught my eye on a previous visit.

For the first time in a long time, I feel that familiar thrum of excitement shivering up my backbone. I think of new paint and fresh, creamy sheets of drawing paper and the dry, sharp smell of new pencil lead, freshly shaven.

It's a new day, and I've been given a new chance. I'm not going to waste a minute of it.

AUTHOR'S NOTE

Part of the fun of writing a story is in the details. While playing the role of storyteller, you are in charge of which are put in and which are left out. This novel is a work of fiction, so none of the storyline is true nor are any of the characters based on real people.

Some historical details in this book surrounding the Abenaki people, however, are true. The Vermont Eugenics project mentioned was a real life event: tragic and heartbreaking and ugly though it was. More than 200 Abenaki were sterilized during the years of 1931 to 1941, and individuals from this particular ethnic group were not the only victims. More information about the nationwide Eugenics Project can be found in this study: *Eugenics: Compulsory Sterilization in 50 American States* (http://www.uvm.edu/~lkaelber/eugenics/).

There also have been residential locations in and around Franklin County, Vermont, where Abenaki burial grounds have been uncovered.

And finally, after many years the Abenaki Nation at Missisquoi received official recognition by the State of Vermont on May 7, 2012.

.

ABOUT THE AUTHOR

J.P. Choquette has been writing professionally since 2007. Published in a number of national and regional magazines, journals and newspapers, she fulfilled a lifelong dream and wrote her first novel, *Epidemic*, which was published in 2013. She's a member of Sisters in Crime, a national organization for mystery writers and is currently at work on a third suspense novel.

She and her family live in Vermont.

Visit Scared E Cat (www.scaredEcat.com) to learn more, sign up for the author's newsletter, and connect with other readers and writers of great suspense.

Made in the USA
Charleston, SC
01 March 2014